A DOOR TO ANYWHERE

PEP CLUBB

ISBN: 978-1-4669-9924-4 (sc)
ISBN: 978-1-4669-9925-1 (e)

Trafford rev. 06/07/2013

 www.trafford.com

North America & international
toll-free: 1 888 232 4444 (USA & Canada)
phone: 250 383 6864 ♦ fax: 812 355 4082

CHAPTER 1

George L. Pepper, was lying on his death bed, at his home, at Stony Knob North Carolina!

He drifted in and out of a coma, (at 90 years) his life unfolded before him at the moment he was thinking of his beautiful wife Mary, and their life together!

She had died at the age of 85, but the love he felt for her, would never die.

He met her in school, at Duke University, she was studying to be a Doctor and he to be a Lawyer!

And after all the schooling, they had worked for 15 years, both their families had died, and left them 10 million dollars!

Mary wanted to travel, so they both sold their practice's, they started touring in the United States, after they traveled to all the State's in the U.S. they toured Canada, and from there to South America, but they would fly home to Ashville N.C. and to Stony Knob, between Travel's, to make sure Wayne and Ethel were all right!

Wayne and Ethel were the caretakers, of their home and lived on the property!

There next trip, took them to Europe, after visiting all the countries Europe

They ended up in London, Mary was becoming a pack rat, buying things and shipping them home to Stony Knob!

And George like to tease her about being one, They found themselves at an Antique shop one day, that Mary just had to visit, after rambling all over the shop!

The owner invited them to check the warehouse in the back of the shop, that the shop had been in his family for six generations, and Mary wanted to browse around in there to!

They were rummaging around in the Warehouse for a good hour, when George discovered something covered with dust, leaning against the wall, George "ask the owner of the shop if he had a brush," and the Owner gave him one, and he burshed away a quarter inch of dust, from what looked like a shield carved on a door!

And what he saw engraved on the shield were the words written in Latin!

(A DOOR TO ANYWHERE)

When he saw that he called Mary over to look at it, when she saw it, she took the brush from George, and started uncovering another part of the door. It was engraved with what looked like ivy leaves all over the rest of the door, Mary smiled at George, and said "I've just got to have this," she called the shop owner over and ask," "what do you want for this old door?"

He scratched his bald head, smiled "I've never noticed it before, but it's got to be real old, what will you pay for it?"

And that's when the haggling started, Mary "offered him a thousand dollars for it," and he didn't cave in until she reached 35 hundred!

And of course he took that amount!

The crating and shipping, it back to the U.S., cost another 5 hundred dollars, George smiled at her "honey I'm not sure you got a good deal at that price!"

She kissed him, "oh but I did, and you will think so tonight." And George did think she got a very good deal, after the night she gave him!

They stayed two week, in London, and were ready to go back home, to Stony knob! To check on Wayne and Ethel, when they got home, it would be a stop over, they were going to Florida, it was still pretty cold in the mountain's, they tried to get Wayne and Ethel, to go to the Sun Shine State with them!

But Wayne said "the Missus and I are snug as a bug in a rug right here!"

So George and Mary went to Palm Beach, with out them, George and Mary owned a condo and usually stayed there in the Winters months!

Mary didn't get to see her door, until late Spring, the trees had leafed out and the weather was just right, warm in the daytime, and cool at night, George and Mary, were gald to be home, Mary got busy planting flowers in every pot around the place, Ethel already had all kinds of flowers, around the house!

George found the old door and cleaned it up, when he finished with all the oil and waxing, it was a beautiful thing to behold, to George it seemed to have something magical about it!

He measured the door and it was to large to put anywhere in the house, so he got some 4x4's to frame the door in, and finished the wood and had ivy craved and stained to look like the old door, then mounted the old door into its new frame, then put four inch casters, to mount on the two cross bars holding up the frame!

It was a thing to behold, when he showed it to Mary, she was so excited, as she was looking at the shield on the door and the words engraved on it, she turned and smiled at George and pointed at the shield! "Have you noticed under the large letters, of the Door to Anywhere!"

George got a magnifying glass, started looking and sure enough there were smaller writing!

Mary said "we will have to get dental picks and stiff burshes to be able to make out what it says."

George laughed "I knew my eye sight was getting bad, I thought it was just a rough texture over the rest of the sheild!"

Mary put her arms around George, said "love I'm taking you to the eye Doctor tomorrow." They both chuckled at that!

Over the next four weeks, they cleaned the letters, to reveal what they were telling them, George and Mary worked on the Latin for a month before they could figure out what it said!

The day they figured it out, they both stared at each other for a long time, Mary spoke first "honey what does this mean?"

George replied "it sound like we have something, that belonged to the old Magician (Merlin) you remember the story, the tale of King Arther and the knights of the round table!"

"WOW" Mary said "wait a minute I thought that was just a story that was passed down through the ages, a story for young boys."

George "I know love, I read it when I was a boy, and wished I could be a knight in shinning armor! Wait! I did find my beautiful maiden!"

George took her into his arms, and was fondling all her many charms, and they finished the deed of love, as lover have done sence the beginning of time!

The next morning, after breadfast, after showering and getting ready for the day. Mary ask "George if they were going to try the door out today!"

George replied "why not, love," so they went to the basement!

As Mary approached it she read what it said!

MERLIN'S ESCAPE
A DOOR TO ANYWHERE

This Door I created from King Arther's round table, after the fall of Camelot! My kind of magic seems to be fading into the past this is proof that I was alive, as was King Arther, this door has been my escape many times—the person who possess this door

can go any where they desire! at its destination it will
be invisible to all but the one who possess it! it will
attach it self to the wall at a destination you desire!
this is the last bit of Magic that I possess! as I'm sure I
will pass into Legend and fade into the past!
MERLIN!

Mary seemed to feel cautious, she ask, George "if they should try this?"

Georg smiled "well love, I don't think it will do anything! I think it's just something from the past, that we find beautiful and I will display it any where in our home and be very proud to display it! George lifted the old latch and pulled the door open, and to their surprise, when it was completely opened it looked dark and cloudy and forbidding! They both looked at each other, and they both were spooked by what they saw, George rolled it away from the wall, and they both walked around the door and they couldn't see through the door!

Mary laughed to herself, said "we are the possessor's of this door!"

Where do we want to go? Mr. George Pepper." George shut the door and said "lets go somewhere simple, let go to out bedroom!"

He shut the door, when he opened it, they walked into their bedroom, and on a wall that had no door, was Merlin Door! George and Mary dance around their bedroom, at being able to do what just happened!

And from that day forward, George and Mary had a blast, going from place to place!

They both liked to play, slot machines, so they went from Casino to Casino!

Las Vegas, Atlantic City, Tunica, all the one's in the States, and the Islands.

The one Mary liked most was Monte Carlo on the French Rivera, they dined all over the World!

When they reached their mid seventies, they began to slow down. Mary was slowing down fast, George watched over her like a parent would a child.

George, took her to every medical specialist, but they all said "she was just getting older, and told him he was to, that they both should just slow down!"

So they only used it once a week, then once a Month, until Mary at the age of 85 died, and George was left alone!

He grieved for almost 2 years, until he met a showgirl at the Flamingo Hilton in Las Vegas, who looked like his Mary!

He wined and dined her for almost a month, until she wore him out sexually then he realized he was 87 years old, and that he wasn't a kid anymore so he never went there again!

But now and again he would think about all things she had done to him, and he would smile to himself, and think WOW!

He started thinking about what he would do with all he and Mary had accumulated during their lifetime together!

They were not able to have any children, and he didn't want to leave it all to the State!

So he started looking for relatives and he got his old Law Firm, which were handling all his Legal work!

The firm started looking on Mary's side of the family, for living relatives, but they couldn't find any that were still living. So he instructed them to check on his side of the family, they came back to him, that there was a Gary Pepper, living in Stanley, N. C. that was his great nephew on his Father's, that he was Gary's great Uncle, George had them to check on his Nephew they found all of Gary's records, they discovered he was married to Janice W. Pepper and that they had 2 grown children, and 3 grandchildren, and that they were retired, with a modest retirement income!

CHAPTER 2

At first he thought about visiting his Nephew, to see if he liked him, and also to see if he could handle Merlin's door!

After he and Mary found out just what the door was, a magical door, that was created in ancient times by someone, who was supposed to be fictional but who had lived, and was almost more than he and Mary could handle at first!

They found all the reading material, on the subject they could find. It took them some time to figure out all the Latin words, and realized that King Arther and Merlin were real people, who lived in the past!

Mary at first wanted to write a book on all they had learned on the subject of King Arthur and Merlin, and that they had the proof with the door!

After they traveled through the door for a while, they knew they couldn't tell the world!

Because it would be something every Government in the World would want to take from them!

That people would kill to possess it!

George and Mary built a large walk in closet, behind a floor to sealing 7 foot mirror, which was in fact a vault!

All their cloths was there to, Mary wanted it, so she could dress for their trips!

They swore themselves to keep it a secret for their own safty, for the rest of there lives!

George wrote an 8 page brief on Merlin's door, and put it in a locked brief case along with his new will for his nephew, Gary!

Because the time of his death, he thought would be soon, his health was failing fast!

After two years his body, started breaking down, his Doctors told his body was just wearing out! they put him in bed for a while, but he didn't like it at all, but he wasn't able to stay out of it for long, he had a staff of nurses, doctors checking on him every day!

So on a Tuesday, a cold February morning, George Lenoard Pepper died at 7:45 a.m., with a smile on his face, dreaming he was in bed with his beautiful Mary, doing what they had done so many times in their live's making love!

Ashville and the surrounding, communities, morned the passing of Mr. George Lenoard Pepper, who had given a lot of money, for many causes in the surrounding area, in to the State!

The Governor of the State of North Carolina gave the eulogy at his funereal!

There were notices in the local papers, that there were no heirs to the Pepper Fortune, but his Law Firm, assured them that there was an heir to his Estate.

At the request of Mr. Pepper, they be notified, three weeks after his Funereal!

At the Law Firm of Pucker, Packer and Hacker!

Mr. Leroy Hacker was given the responsibilities, to consolidate Mr. Pepper's Estate, when that was done, and the Law Firm had taken a large chunk of change from the Estate, there was 15 million and a house at stony knob, to go to Mr. Gary Norman Pepper!

At exactly three weeks after George Pepper died, the Law Firm of Pucker, Packer and Hacker sent a letter to Mr. Gary Pepper at 101 Taylor Rd. in Stanley North Carolina, to inform him that he had inherited the Estate of Mr. George Lenoard Pepper!

That he needed to come to their offices, to hear the reading of his will, And gave him the address where they were located!

Gary had just got through cutting his grass, at 101 Taylor Rd., he and his wife lived in his wife's old home place, by a railroad track, just out side Stanley N. C., at first he loved the old home place, but over the years he had grown to hate, living there, Janice's Mother had built two room, and later her Dad and her Mother's brothers added two more rooms and a bathroom and a back porch and a front porch!

The best thing about it for him was it was paid for and with a modest retirement income! they could enjoy themselves, with almost anything they wanted in life!

He rode the lawnmower to the mail box, and got the mail, there was just one letter and the rest was just junk mail, he rode the mower back to the house and was in the process of putting the mower away! when he pulled the mail from his pocket, he noticed the letter from the Law offices of Pucker, Packer and Hacker!

And after reading the return address he chuckled at their names, Pucker, Packer and Hacker!

He noticed the letter was stamed (Urgent Open Immediately) after seeing that he wondered why some Ashville Attorneys, would want to send him a letter!

He knew he hadn't done anything in that part of the mountains. he and his Wife, liked to go to the Indian Casino in Cherokee "Harrahs" they loved to play the slots!

And would get up there once or twice a month, up I-40 they had to go through Ashville, and he couldn't remember ever stopping there he hoped he wasn't any kind of trouble!

He opened the envelope to see just what it was about, and to his surprise, they wanted him to come up to their offices! that "he had inherited the Estate of his Great Uncle the late George Lenoard Pepper!"

He was a little skeptical about what he was reading, he didn't know any George Pepper!

All the Pepper's he knew and had known in his life, were dead except for his own family!

But in the letter there was a toll free number to call as soon as possible he looked at his watch it was only 3:30 p.m. so he went into the house, Smiling at his wife, he said "talking about your rich uncle dieing in the poor house and leaving, us million dollars"!

He gave her the letter. And went to the phone and dialed the number in the letter!

He was routed to the office of a Mr. Hacker, when he answered the phone, Gary "introduced himself," Mr. Hacker said "Gary we need you in our offices, as soon as you can arrange it!

Gary said "I'm sorry, but do you have the right person. I've never know a George Pepper!"

Mr. Hacker answered, "sir we know that. When can you come up?"

Gary ask "what time do you want me there?"

Mr. Hacker replied "would 1: 00 p.m. tomorrow be ok with you?"

Gary "let me run this by my wife, hang on a moment," Gary called his wife Janice, and said "a Mr. Hacker wants to see us in his office tomorrow at 1:00 O'clock, what do you think!"

Janice ask "will it be worth our time?" Gary heard Mr. Hacker chuckle into the phone! then he said "ask her if 15 million would get her here!"

Gary said "holy cow" and peed in his pants, and said "Mr. Hacker we will be there!" $$$$$ holy! $$$$$$ cow ! $$$$$$$$$$$$$$$$$$$$$$$$$$$$$$$

Mr. Hacker said "let me give you the direction on how to get here, and if you should get lost, we will come and get you sir!"

Gary said "would you please repeat those directions to my wife! I'm a little shaken at the moment and I need to clean myself up." Hacker said "why sure Mr Pepper."

Gary gave the phone to Janice, with tears in his eyes, and a pee stain on his pants!

Janice looked strangly at him, and said "what's this all about Knuckle head!"

He smiled and said "ask him" then left the room to change his pants, he dried his eyes, when he got back, Janice had done the same thing only there was a little brown stain along with the pee in her panties, and large crocodile tears streaming down her face, he took her by the hand and lead into the bathroom, gave her a towel and said "honey I know how you feel and after you clean youself up!"

"We need to call the kids," Janice said "I'm not sure we can drive ourselves," then she started laughing, "this is great, I can't wait to tell to tell them about this." "Well while your cleaning youself up I'm going to call (Broomer) their daughter, Sabrina," (ha! ha!) Janice said OH NO YOUR NOT!

He said "well I am, and you can call (Buster) their son Gary Jr. is that alright?" Yes she said! Gary asked her "do you want to wait until you've cleaned up, or do you want the cell phone?" She replied get me the cell in here now!

He did as he was instructed, like he always did! He got the cell from the kitchen and gave it to her, then went into the living room, sat down and called his daughter, the phone, Brent answered, Gary said "I have good news! You Don't have to go to work tomorrow!"

Brent chuckled "that sounds like a plan to me! Brent gave the phone to Sabina, she said" hi old man, what's up! Papa replied "well young lady, you don't have to go to work tomorrow! And if you so desire, never again! she said "(WOW) that sounds good to me, but just how am I going to do that?'

Papa said "you know the old story about my rich uncle who died in the poor house and left me a million dollars!

Only honey it's 15 million! "WOW" she said "when did you find out?" Papa replied "I found out about thirty minutes ago, and we have to be at the Lawyers office at 1:00 P.M. tomorrow, you or your brother will have to drive us up to Ashville. Or Brent could do if he wants to?" Broomer said I "I bet he would like to drive," Papa are your sure! Papa replied well old grill we will know tomorrow!"

"But it sure sounds like, were all going to have 5 million apiece, and don't that sound wonderful to you!" Sabrina said "holy cow, I just peed in my pants!" Papa laughed "that's exactly what you Mother and I both did when we heard the news!"

"Sabrina your Mother is in the bathroom cleaning herself while were talking, she made me get the cell phone for her, so she could call your brother!"

Sabrina Started laughing, and said I'll bet that was a sight to see!

Papa could hear Brent talking in the back ground, and she said "were rich!" then said "sorry Papa, Brent wanted to know what was going on!" Papa said "we need to be there at 1:00 o'clock, why don't we make a morning of it by eating breakfast on the road! Wait a minute your Mother wants to talk to you." he gave the phone to her." Janice started laughing, "did your Papa tell what we both did," Janice laughed again, you did" well your brother did to! That make all of doing the same thing!"

Sabrina laughed and ask "what time should we be ready tomorrow?"

Janice told her, "how about 8:30 or 9:30," Sabrina replied what about 9:00 o'clock, we can come pick you up, then go pick up Gary, and that should put us in Ashville about 11:30, even if we stop for breakfast somewhere."

Janice "that would be fine, but hang on, let me run that by you Dad? he said "that would be fine, because he didn't think he would get much sleep tonight!"

Thinking about being a rich man! Janice "Broomer, I think he's gone slap crazy, He's dancing around in the kitchen now! And "I think I'll join your Father!"

He doing more than just dancing and I'm the one he dose that with him!"

"Bye"

When they were thorugh, they both were contented and happy, it was only 5 p, m. in the afternoon, when they got up out of bed!

CHAPTER 3

The phone rang, Janice answered it, she smiled at Gary, and said, "he's **r**ight here." gave the phone to Gary, "he said Hi! Mr. Hacker, I guess you know you've just turned our world, up side down!"

Hacker chuckled, "I though so! he told Gary that he owned a Limousine and a driver that is on your payroll. And I think it would be best if Roland came and picked you up, with your family, and he could take you to Stony Knob, when were through, with the reading of the will!" there are key's for the house, and the cars here in our office!"

Gary "I hadn't thought about a house, involved in the will, and what about a limo? How many people will it hold?"

Mr. Hacker said "I think it would hold eight people comfortably!"

There will be only 6 of us tomorrow, there are 3 Grandchildren, but they will be in school, and I don't want to bother them just yet about any of this. what time should we be ready for Roland?"

Mr. Hacker "what about 10 o'clock, that should get you here around 12:30, and that should be good for us!"

Gary "we were thinking, we would eat brakefast, on the road, could he be here by 09:30 and I'll have my crowd here at my house at that time, and Roland want have to run over the place, picking us up!"

Mr. Hacker "Mr, Pepper we know exactly where you live. and Roland has a GPS unit in the Limo! Hacker "Gary we'll see you tomorrow!"

Gary "thanks Mr. Hacker," Hacker he replied, "think nothing of it, you have a good day!"

Gary hung up the phone, "honey call the kids, back and tell them to be here at the house by 9 o'clock, we're going to be picked up by our Limousine, a guy by the name of Roland is driving us to the meeting and apparently he works for me, or will be after the reading of the will! (WOW) Honey that almost to much!"

Janice smiled at him, then said "I think you can handle it old man," and gave him a bear hug and a kiss, Gary smiled "maybe I'm not through with just yet young lady!"

Janice was on the phone, talking to the kids, she told "them to be here at the house by 9 O'clock," and they both agreed to be there with bell on!

It was 11 p.m. before Gary finally got to sleepy enough to go to bed, when head hit the pillow he was gone!

Gary didn't get up until 7:30 a.m. the next morning, Janice had to pull him out of bed to get ready for their big day, Gary shaved, took a bath, then ask his wife "what to ware for a reading of a will?"

Janice said "your silly, just ware something comfortable, you know we're eating breakfast on the road, I think Shoney's in Morganton would be the beat place to eat!"

Gary "sounds like a winner to me sugerbabe!

They were ready to go by 8:30, when the kids got there, they both seemed very happy and excited to be going with us, Gary Jr. said "Papa you don't know just how happy, I'm going to be, walking away from that place I'm working!"

Gary Sr. "I think I do son, I've worked at a few places that I didn't want to work at, but I had to, for your Mom and you knuckle heads, but somehow I finally made it to retirement, and I'm sure you would have made it to, but now you can coast as long as you like, and only work if you want to. but I would advise you to make money off the money we get, so you and your children want have to struggle, like I did, when I was growing up, but as I think of it, your Mom and I are getting along fine now, we could get most anything we wanted or needed, right Mother!"

Janice said "yes, and were happy, your Father and I think both of you kids have made a good life for youselfs!"

Broomer laughed "your right, but things are about to get better, right Brent?"

Sherry "that's for sure, they both chuckled at that!"

Just then a long black Cadillac Limousine, pulled off the road and into their driveway!

Gary Jr. said "(WOW) Pops that's one sharp ride you got there!"

Gary Sr. smiled "well son if your good, I might just let you borrow it on a Saturday night!

Gary Jr. laughed "sounds like a plan to me Pop!"

Sabrina spoke up "I get it before he dose Papa!" Janice their Mom "now children, were not going to fight over a car!"

Sabrina "Mom I'm just wanted to razz Gary Jr. a little like he does me!"

As they walked out side, Papa locked the front door, not realizing he would never live in the old house, ever again!

When they all got to the Limo, Roland had the door, Gary Sr. walked up to Roland and shook his hand, and introduced himself, and his family, Roland seemed pleasant to talk to, Gary Sr. ask Roland "if he had breakfast yet?"

Roland replied that "he had!"

Gary Sr. "we haven't and want to stop I Morganton to eat breakfast, if that alright with you?"

Roland replied "yes sir that's fine with me, as they got out on the road, Roland said "there's a bar with soft drinks if you want one!" Brent found it ask "if anyone wanted one?"

Roland said "he would like a bottle of water," we passed him one, Janice ask "if there was a diet Sun drop," Gary Sr. had one to, they all had some thing to drink!

And it seemed like short ride with all the chatter going on up the road, they were pulling into Shoney's to eat breakfast, as they got out of the car, Gary Sr. ask "Roland if he would like to go eat something with them?"

He replied "no sir, I've got a good book with me and I'll read until your ready to leave!"

They all went into Shoney's and eat breakfast, they were there for a good 30 minutes, talking about Papa's new found wealth, and what it would mean to all of them, Papa chuckled "don't count your chickens juat yet! we don't know how the money is tied up, we may have to liquidate some assets, in order for us to share it, lets just wait and see what the Lawyers have to say, and how the will reads, but you know I've always wanted to be able to do something for you both, all my life, but I thought it would be when we pass on, and you two could sell the old house, and whats left in the Bank!"

"Papa Gary Jr. said "I hope that day is a long way off!"

Gary Sr. said "me to son, but that's the nature of living, one never know when that day will come, but that is why you need to make out will's!"

Janice said "stop talking about dyeing, your not dead until you are!"

They all started laughing!

Broomer said "how did that get started?" Papa "well we are going to a Lawyer's office to hear the reading of my Great Uncle's will!"

Sherry said "look at your watch, we've been talking for over 30 minutes, we better get moving, or what's is name will be leaving us!"

Papa laughed "what's is name, works for me and that car is mine, according to Mr. Hacker!"

"But we've been here a little over 30 minutes, I think we better get going, My watch has 5 after 11:00 and as you know, it's never wrong!" Sabrina and Gary Jr. both held their watche's "we know Papa!"

When he bought his watch, he bought them one to. they all went to the rest room then to the car!

Gary Sr. as they got into the car, "he apologized to Roland," who said "Mr. Pepper, "you need not apologize to me for I work for you! And I've got a really good book and had not noticed the time, and we've got plenty of time!"

Gary Sr. ask "how long will it take us to the Lawyer's offices, Roland "Mr. Pepper, a little over an hour, but I think they'll see you as soon as you get there!"

Gary Sr. smiled "I think your right!" And after eating a good breakfast, they all quiet, Papa had his eye's closed and Mom had her head on his sholder.

Gary Jr. and Sherry had done the same, Sabrina and Brent were giggling, and pointing at them!

And saying something about the way they looked, it must have looked funny to them!

Papa opened his eyes, and said "shush young lady, can't you see were trying rest for a little bit." She replied "yes Father, but it's been a while sense I've seen your eyes closed!

And sometimes you make funny facial features, when your sleeping!"

Papa said I wasn't sleeping, I was just resting my eyes!"

Sabrina laughed again and said "but you were snoring!" He looked at Brent and he shook his head up and down, "yes you did!"

Papa looked at his watch and said "wow I've got 25 after 12:00, I guess I did stack a few Z's, then he ask Roland where they were?"

Roland replied "we're just a few minutes from the Lawyer offices!"

And that seemed to rouse them rest of them, Buster started laughing and said "I guess I went to sleep!"

Brent said "you did, I could feel the vibrations, from your snoring." Brent chuckled and said "I was only kidding, but you did snore!"

Gary Jr. replied, "well I feel refreshed," Sherry said "I do to!" Mom said I feel better to!"

Thay were somewhere in the city of Ashville, and in a few minutes Roland was pulling in front of a 6 story building with a large brass plaque with the words The Law offices of Pucker, Packer and Hacker, Roland was out of the Limo quickly, with the door opened for them!

Roland said "ask for Mr. Hacker at the front desk and the receptionist will direct, where to go, and I'll be in the back parking lot, and they'll know how to contact me there, and good luck!"

They were in the building, quickly, the young lady setting at the desk, said "hi Mr. and Mrs Pepper!"

She smiled "I was the person who found you," she picked up a photograph to show them, him and his wife and one of each of his children, Sabrina and Gary Jr.!

She motion for another girl to come over to cover the desk!

She came around the desk, and hugged them, "I feel like I know you, George gave us the task of finding you, he was the late Mr. Pepper and we all loved him!"

"He was the founder of this Law Firm, now let me take you up stairs to Mr. Hacker's office," she lead them to a bank of elevators and up to the second floor and into Mr. Hacker office!

There were two other Gentleman, setting in the office with another man when they were in the office, the man behind the desk got up, walked over and shook there hands and said "I'm Floyed Hacker these two fellow are the bosses!"

He introduced them, "this is Mr. Pucker and then to Mr. Packer" they, they all shook hands and talked for a bit!

Mr. Pucker said "we'll get out of your way Floyed so you can make these people happy!"

Mr. Hacker said "please follow me!"

They walked into a large conference room, he told them all to have a seat, he then ask Gary Sr. to set at the head of the conference table, the young lady who brought them to the second floor, walked around and opened a door that had a large safe, she opened it, she turned and smiled, at Floyed and said "I forgot it introduce myself down stairs, to the Pepper family!"

He smiled and said "let me introduce you to my lovely wife Ruby, she is the one who found you Gary for the late Georg Pepper, your Great Uncle, Floyed "George talked to me about, when he was a young that he went to a lot of Family reunions, but he could not remember your Father or who he

CHAPTER 4

M arried!" with all the schooling, he had to do at Duke, meeting and marring his Mary!"

"And finishing Law school, they struggled somewhat, with Mary finishing Medical school and they both had to intern to become the successful and professionals they were, She was a very successful heart Doctor, and he a very successful Lawyer, he started this Law Firm, he sold the Practice to Mr Pucker!"

"George and Mary worked for 15 years, until they came into an inheritance, Mary decided she had worked long enough, she wanted to travel, they both sold their practices, and traveled they did!"

"They started in the U.S. and Canada, South America and then to Europe!"

"They were both very generous with their money, if there was a good cause they supported it!"

"I think he wanted to come meet you Gary, you and your family, but his health wouldn't permet that!"

"We liquidated all of his assets per his instruction, you have 15 million in three different Banks, he took out of the folder and handed it ot Gary three Bank books, 5 million in BB&T, 5 million in Bank of America and 5 million in Fidelity Bank, Mr. Pepper paid the inheritance taxes on all the money you are reciving, he did that to keep the State Government and the Federal Government, away from what he is giving you and it totaled up 15 million so you owe no money to them, until the next time!"

"There is a beautiful Estate called Stony Knob, it's on the outskirts of Weverville N. C. and that is yours, he gave him the deed for that plus all the keys for the house!"

"There are two other houses for the staff that maintains the property, Roland lives in one of the houses!"

"Let me tell you the story about the staff, George had two wonderful people who took care of the Estate for years, Wayne and Ethel Moore, George and Mary though of them as family, when Wayne died, Ethel had to be put in a nursing home!"

"George was getting older, so he started looking for help, for Stony Knob, all he could find were Mexican's, he said he wasn't sure about doing it, but he did make sure they were legal and could good English, after a year, he really liked them!"

"he said they have good work ethics, and were fun to be around, he paid them well, there is a trust fund account set up for them to draw their pay from, it's set up under the Stony knob county fund, it's at the People's Bank, that you have to monotor for them, there is 1 and a half million dollars in this account, that you're the steward of this account!"

"The reason the word county is attached to the fund, is for a while the city of Weaverville tried to take in George's estate purely for the taxes!"

"They could get out of him, they weren't going to give him services for his money!"

"Being the astute Lawyer, that he was, he went to the State Legislature in Raleigh, he had enough friends, he got them to pass a law, that his property be declared a county!"

"Thus blocking the City, from taking him in and anyother Cities that thought his property was a plum for picking!"

"He got it passed, and we all thought that bit of legal maneuvering, was a brilliant piece of legal work, and was put in the text books!"

"He was a very smart man!"

Gary smiled "I'm not sure, that I could ever be the kind of person he was!"

Mr. Hacker, smiled "well Gary, George looked you over carefully, he liked what he saw, like I said earlier, when we found you for him, we checked you out and couldn't find anything in you life, negative against you or your family!"

"George thought that given the same circumstances, that he would be just like you!"

"That you were a Pepper and the same blood that ran through his body, ran through your's, he really wanted to meet you and your family, but like I said when his health started failing, it wasn't long before his death. I think that this will, should prove that to you!"

"He set up a trust fund at Duke University, for a million dollars for your Grandchildren, to be divided between Erin, Ben and Luke!"

"He was a graduate from Duke and he wanted to give them that opportunity, but if they don't wish to go to Duke, the money will be transferred to any school they wish to attend!"

"Or at the will of their parents, the money can be given to their children at the age of 21!"

Hacker said "the last thing, are these two brief cases," he pushed them over to Gary, one was almost falt, the other was a good size case, Mr. Hacker said "Gary we don't know what's in them, Mr. Pepper sealed them, before he gave them to us, and you have to sign this release form, that you have been given these Brief cases, and that you've received all to the entitlements of this will!"

Hacker slid the paper in front of Gary Sr. and he signed it, Ruby gave Floyed another form, he said "oh yes this one also, Gary looked at them and smiled at them, then over at his Family as he sighed the paper, and said "I know that me and my faimly will thank my Great Uncle George Lenoard Pepper for the rest of our lives, for this great gift he has given us!"

Gary Sr. stood up and shook the hands of Floyd and Ruby and she hugged him!

And said "I guess your ready to go home!"

He took Janice's hand into his and ask "are you ready to go home Love, she said with tears in her eye's "I am Love"!

Ruby said "I'll call Roland and have him in front, when you get there, and if you ever want to sell Stony Knob, I get first dibs on it!"

Gary looked at her and said "that's a deal!" When they got downstairs, Roland was standing near the door, he ushered them to the car, then he ask Gary Sr. "do you wish to go to Stony Knob? or would you like to eat while we're in town?"

Gary ask "Janice in turn," she ask "the kids" "what they wanted to do," Gary Jr. said "let go to Stony Knob, I want to see it!"

Gary Sr. told "Roland lets go Stony Knob," he replied "yes sir!"

When they were out of Ashville and on their way, Gary Sr. asked "for the brief cases," Brent gave him the large one, he looked at it, "there's a tape on it," he tried to open it, but it was locked, he remembered the envelope with the keys in it, then he ask, "who has the envelope with the keys?"

Sherry said "is this it?" And gave it to him, he poured the key's out and saw one ring of keys he thought would open it!

He borrowed Juniors pocked knife, and sliced through the tape that sealed the case, and the key he selected opened it, and said "Holy Smoke's would you look at this!"

There was a typed written note, on top of the money in the case, he looked around, checking to see if Roland could see, but he was to busy driving.

He set it down on the floor board of the car, for them all to see, then he started reading the note! It reas as follows, "Hi Gary I was hoping we could meet! But it wasn't to be, this case full of money, was a from a condo in West Palm Beach in Florida, Mary and I bought for 9 hundred thousand but when Mary died I sold it for 3 and a half million, and these are the proceeds!"

"When Bob Pucker called and told me they had found you, I gave him thse sealed brief case, along with another smaller case that you might find strange, or alarmed by what you read! But be assured that it's not! Mary and I enjoyed it, just as soon as we discovered what it could do!

And take care of Stony Knob for me!"

P.S.

There are few more page's to this note, that will explain this mistry to you!"

Gary looked at Janice and whispered into her ear, "there is 3 and a half million in that case!"

Then he asked "who has the other brief case?" Broomer gave him it to him, he cut the seal, and opened the case, there were two folders in side, he opened one of the folders, there were pictures of George and Mary taken all over the world, Janice said "they were a good looking couple together, I think you look just like him!"

Then he opened the other folder, there were 8 typed pages, the caption read "Merlin Door"

Gary "there is a safe in my bedroom, behind a large floor to ceiling mirror that contans an old door, (framed and on casters) that belonged to Merlin the Magician, the legend of King Auther, and the Knights of the round table!

Mary and I were in London, at the end of our tour of Eruope, we were in an old antiqie shop that had been in the same family for 6 generations we talked the owner of the shop into letting us browse in the back storage area of the shop!"

"That's when we found the old door, I could make out the writing, it was carved in Latin, I could read what it said, the words read "A Door to anywhere!"

"That intrigued me. I showed it to Mary, and she fell in love with it and she bought it, at to high a price. We shipped it home, and we didn't look at it again until late spring to the following year, after we cleaned it up, and deciphered what was written on it, that Merlin had created it from Arthur's round table, after the fall of Camelot!"

That he who possesses this door it can take you to anywhere the possessor desires to go!"

"You will think I'm out of my mind, but it's all true, Mary wanted to write a book about it, and tell the world the truth about Merlin and Arthur, that they did exist!"

That this door proved it!"

"But after we talked about it, we thought about taking it on tour with the book. She would write about it, but after we used it, we soon realized that people in power, be it Government, or people with very large amounts of money, would take it or kill us for it!"

"We believed for our own safety, that it should remain our Secret!" As for you Gary, you should let it remain our secret also!"

Stony Knob, is a beautiful place to live, and as large as it is I think you and your family could live there and be very happy!"

After reading the pages, Gary said "wow"!

Janice looked at him, "what's the matter love." Gary looked at all of them, shrugged his sholder's and gave the papers to his wife, "your going to have read this to!"

Just as they she finished reading the papers, they pulled into a private drive way!

Janice gave the note back to Gary, she said "what dose this mean honey?"

Gary looked at her, "beats me love, we'll have to wait and see!"

Roland stopped at a large black ornamental gate and when they opened, he drove through, they entered a large court yard in front of a very large two story house, that was covered with rock!

To Gary it was the most beautiful place, he had ever seen. Roland drove the car around to the house on a circular driveway!

He stopped in front at a large double doorway, he turned smiling "this is Stony Knob, Mr. Pepper, your home!"

For a few moments, no one moved, just looking at the house!

Roland had already opened the doors, before they finally got out of the car when they did they spread out in front of the house, talking to each other, about how beautiful the house was!

CHAPTER 5

Gary Jr. turned and told his Father, "that he was going to live here to, Sabrina said "me to Papa," Janice had her arm around Gary Sr., and said I know you are, this house is big enough for all of us!"

Roland walked over to Gary and said "my wife Maria will have you some thing to eat and show you the house! I will put the car away and join you shortly!"

Gary shook his hand "thanks Roland, we'll see you later, then Gary ask him if there was any other cars in the garage?"

There was a five bay garage with the doors closed, that set next to the two lovely cottages!

Roland replied, "yes sir there are two Beamers (BMW's) plus the Cadillac I thought the Lawyer gave me three sets of keys!"

Before he got away from Roland, his crowed was already in the front door. when he got inside, Maria was already talking to them, she had introduced herself to them, Janice was introducing all of them to Maria, as I walked Janice said "this is my husband Gary Sr." Maria seemed like such a nice person!

We all felt at home at once, Maria ask "are you hungry, or would you like a tour of the house first?"

Janice "lets tour first," Maria took them from the foyer to main suite of room's, that had belonged to George and Mary! these rooms were large and full of old world antiqies, but they were all decorated very well and clean!

There was a den or a faimly room full of leather couches and chairs with a large fire place, and a large flat screen television!

With bookshelves all around the room, and they were full of books, Junior

"Pop this would be a very good reading room!"

Gary Sr. replied "your so right about that son, it sure beats having to the local Library, I'll bet this thing has ever subject, you could think about reading!"

Then Maria took them into the bedroom, Janice "I really like this!" there was a couch, two chairs, in the corner of the room, with a large king size bed!

Maria "Mr. Pepper left instructions that this room be refurbished, after his death!"

Janice thought it looked like the chairs, had been reupholstered, the bedding and drapes had been changed!

Maria said "in the large closet, we took out the old style clothing, and had the ones we thought you would want to keep, drycleaned, and they are still hanging in the closet, but if you want them removed, we can take them out later!"

Maria showed them the inside of it, Janice pointed at the Mirror for Gary to see, Gary "honey I saw it when we came into the room," it was the largest closet, they had ever seen, it was as big as two of their rooms at home, there were a lot of cloths hanging in there, and all in plastic bags,!

Maria smiled Janice "I think you could wear them just fine!" As Maria started to lead them out of the bedroom and back into the den, but Brent was looking out of the two double French doors, he said "you guys have to see this, there is a terrace, and it has a very beautiful view!"

Maria "oh I forgot," then lead them back to the terrace, and through the doors, Maria said "in the spring and summer, this is so beautiful," there were pots full of beautiful flowers, and Wicker furniture, under a covered porch!

The view was perfect, and you could see in the distance a town, Gary Sr. ask Maria, "what town is that?"

Maria replied "Weverville sir," Gary Sr. said "I guess you guys know who owns this part of the house, it belongs to your Mother!"

Maria smiled and said "the other two suties are much like this one, there may be some small differences, and each suite has its own laundry room and is furnished with everything you would need!"

She lead them out of the bedroom and back into the den, Maria chuckled and said "there is a game room, you need to see, first, before we go to the other two suites, it just off the den, and I'm sure you will love it, when they walked into it, there was a pool table, two card tables, and all around the room were shelves filled with all kinds of games, Broomer was looking all around the room, Sabrina said "Papa, were going to have a lot of fun in here!"

Papa hugged her, "you bet we will," when Maria got their attention again She ask "if they were ready to go see the other two suites and after they viewed the other part of the house, Sabrina clained the suite of room on the right side of the house, and Gary Jr. wanted the upstairs rooms and they both were pleased!

Maria took them to the dinning room, "told them to have a seat, that she would get them something to eat," Janice ask "if there was a table in the kitchen, where we could all eat?"

Maria "yes Mam, "but you might, be more comfortable in here!"

Janice, "we've all worked, all our lives, but now we've retired, I retired the nursing field, my daughter, Sabrina is still in nursing," Sabrina, held up a finger, "Mom, that was in nursing, past tense, I've just retired!"

Brent smiled, "me to!"

Gary Jr. chuckled "well I guess, I could quit to!" he had just changed jobs and didn't like it at all!

Maria "well, there is enough room, sometimes we all eat in the big house, Roland and I have two boy's, Hector and Rosie have two girls, they all go to school in Weaverville, in the summer, Roland puts them to work here at Stony Knob!"

"When Mr. Pepper hired us, he put Roland in charge of Stony Knob. when he needed more help, Roland hired Hector and Rosie, and with the children helping, we can maintain the place well!"

"In the last day's of Mr. Pepper's life, it was easer to feed everyone here, "so please follow me," they went through a swinging door into the kitchen, as they entered, Sherry said "wow what a great Kitchen." Maria "it's a state of the arts kitchen, when Mrs. Pepper was a live, she held some great parties in this house! She was a wonderful person to work for!"

"I told Roland, that he should have everyone here to meet the new owners."

Just as she said that, Roland came in with two healthy young boy's and two attractive young girl's, behind the children were two adult's!

Roland introduced them, he started with the boy's first, "this is Joe, our oldesd, who is 16 teen and a very bright young man!"

"This is Todd our baby, who is 14 teen, we think he might be smarter than his older brother!"

"And this Hector, my very best friend, and his wife Rosie, and the two young ladies are Betty, she's 14 teen and Jane is 15 teen, and according to their grades in school they are smarter than the boy's!"

As the were introduced they went around shaking hands with the Pepper family members!

And when they all, finished eating together, they all pitched in and cleaned the kitchen!

Roland and Hector with their family's, went to their home's!

And the Pepper family, went to the den, and started talking about getting on with their live's!

Gary Sr. had left the two brief case's under their bed in their siute, but, he brought them from the bedroom and laid them on the table in front of the couches and opened one of the cases and started stacking money on the table, in 1 million stacks, he pushed one stack in front of Sabrina and one in front of Gary Jr., then "Oh yes, the bank accounts!"

He pulled the Bank books out of the envelopes, and gave one to Gary Jr. and one to Sabrina!

"Tomorrow we need to go to these Bank's and put your names under mine, as Administrator of these accounts, I talked to the Lawyer, about putting these accounts in your names, but he said "if I gave it to you now, you would have to pay taxes on it now!"

But the way to get around that is to let you administer, the accounts, so at tax time, we all take care of the taxes!"

He smiled "dose that bother you guys, to do it that way!"

Sabrina and Gary Jr. smiled and said "no Pop, not at all, Gary Sr. chuckled and said "that's 6 million, 5 hundred thousand for me and you guy's get 6 million each, Do you think we're rich yet?" Gary Jr. said "you know, I had completely forgot about my son," Sherry "I'm not sure, I want to change his school!"

Janice "they only have one more year, so we should get them into a good prep school, so they would be ready for Duke!

"The money is already there for them, we should check into that!"

Papa "I think there is enough room for the kids in your suites, Brent "we have to go get them, there expecting us back home today!"

Janice "I don't have anything to sleep in tonight!"

Papa smiled "you want need anything to sleep in tonight, I don't think I'll let you sleep at all to night love!"

The Kid's laughed at that, Junior "that sounds like a winner to me to Pop."

Sabrina "how are we going to get the kids?"

Gary Sr. "there's two beamers in the garage, and of coarse the Limo, So I think were going back down the hill this afternoon!"

Janice "are you going to show them what's in the vault?"

Gary Sr. then got the other brief case pulled out the information on what he and Janice had read. "I think maybe you should all read this!" He gave it to Sabrina and Brent, they started reading, when they finished, Sabrina gave to to Gary Jr. and Sherry!

Sabrina was shaking her her head along with Brent, "no way that this could be true!"

Sherry started shaking he head no! Gary Jr. "if this is true, it would be earth shaking wow!"

Papa "lets go check it out. When they got into their bedroom and into the closet!

They started looking, how to open the Vault, Papa remembered something in the envelope with the keys, "wait a minute," I'll be right back, he went into the den and retrieved the envelope!

When he got back, he took out of the envelope a small remote control. He said "Ha Haw" pointed it at the mirror and it opened inwardly, the lights came on in the Vault!

And all around the Vault were shelves. Displaying the most beautiful, sparkling, array of Jewelry!

When they saw it, Papa said, "Holy cow, would you just look at that!"

Everyone started picking up pieces and admiring them, Sabrina "I want this," Brent "that thing is a good four or five carrots of diamonds." Janice "wait a minute young lady, I think you could borrow it, but I claiming all of this!"

Janice had a big smile on her face, and Jr. started opening drawers on the bottom half of the Vault, he remarked "well, well, would you look at this!"

A drawer, full of watches, expensive ones at that!"

Brent starte picking them up and said, "these are very expensive watches!"

Everyone was ignoring the door, that was standing in the center of the Vault!

Papa was admiring the art work on the door, it was carved with ivy leafs and in the center was a sheld, with some kind of writing on it, Dad finely "hey you people, this is what we came to see!"

They all stopped looking at the loot in the Vault, and came over and was admiring the beauty and the craftsmanship of the door!"

Gary Sr. decided to open it, he pulled the latch up, and it opened, and it was dark and cloudy and forbidding!

CHAPTER 6

Sherry "what the heck is that thing?" Junior walked aroud it. He said "Pop this is a mystery!" Papa "do you knuckle heads, not remember what you read a few minutes ago!"

"This is the door my Great Uncle, our gracious benefactor, was talking about, his instruction on how to use this door!"

He that possesses this door can go anywhere, and where do we want to go!

"Your Mother said she need's something to sleep in and both of you need to get your children, and where did you leave your cars?"

Stanley. Do you want to go to Stanley?"

They were looking at their Father strangely, "do we all agree we want to go the Pepper house?"

He opened the door, and they all could see the inside of their Mother's bedroom!

For a good minute they didn't move until, there Mother stepped into her old bedroom, and motioned to them to follow her!

When they finely walked through the door, they were looking at each other strangely wondering what they just did!

When they looked back at their Father, he was still in the Mountains waving at them, through the door! Then he stepped into the room with them, "is this Magic or what!"

Then he shut the door, to Sabrina, Brent, Gary Jr. and Sherry, it disappeared Sabrina "well I guess we have to ride back up to the mountains!"

Papa replied, well honey, "he who possesses the door, can see it!"

Then he ask "Janice if she could still see it?" She "of course," then she turned to them and said "you can't see it!"

"But it's still there, your Father and I can see it clearly!"

Junior looked at his Mom and Dad, "when Papa closed the door it disap-peared!"

She looked at Gary Sr., smiled "well honey it's still there." she told "Papa to open the door for them!"

When he opened the door, it became visible to them again !

He noticed he had left the door to the Vault open, he walked back into it and shut the Vault door, he walked back into their old bedroom, he ask if anyone wanted to go back and do it again!"

At first nobody moved, then Brent walked back into the Vault, then back into their old bedroom of the house in Stanley!

Then he said "do you know how muck money we could make by selling tickets, to do this!"

Sabrina held up the Bank book "why should we?"

Papa chuckled "this door and this information, Uncle George left us should remain our secret!"

"I think you all know if this got out, and into the wrong hands we could be in big trouble, because I think people would kill to have it in their possesson you guys think about that, say you wanted to go fishing anywhere in the world your Mom or I could let you go in the morning, and we could, open the door in the evening, or make arrangement for a time to meet you, at a designated area!"

Say your Mother and I wanted to go to Las Vegas, we could go in the morni-ng and come back at night, or spend as much time as we choose to stay!"

Papa smiled "I'm getting excited just thinking about it!

Janice said "honey we have to go get the kids!"

Papa "sorry I just got carried away, thinking about being able to take a trip like that!"

He ask "how are we doing this, cars or door?

"It's your choice. Sabrina "Papa take me to my house, I want to try it one more time!"

Sherry "we're going to," Janice spoke up "let me get something to sleep in!"

Then she got a travel bag, loaded it up, and said "well I'm ready to go Papa"

Gary Sr. smiled "rats I was hoping to keep you naked all night long!"

Janice smiled "you wished," Junior started laughing and it spread to them all!

Papa his face a little red "well I guess we're ready to go!"

He opened the door, and they all walked into the Messer household. Sherry

"WOW this is great," Erin was in her bedroom, Ben was at his computer, when they heard the noise in the house, they came quickly!

Ben wanted to know how did you guys get in the house, with out me seeing you drive up?"

Brent "that's a long story, pack a few thing's together, for the next few days your coming with us!"

With in twenty minutes, they both were ready to leave!

Erin was standing at the front door, "she said "just how are we getting there I don't see any cars in front of the house!"

Papa looked at the rest of them "Ok I didn't think about the kid's knowing!"

Broomer "I know what you mean, we could put blindfolds over their eye's,"

Janice said "I don't like the thoughts of that, there will be more questions if we do it that way!"

Papa "well Babe do you want to try explain it to them?"

"I won't let them play with it, as I'm sure they will want to when they find out just what it will do, and they must keep it a secret to, you think they can do that?"

Brent "we should put blind folds over their eye's for sure!" they called them into the kitchen with the rest of them, Brent told Ben and Erin that this going to be strange to you! Were going to Uncle Gary's to pick up Luke, but first we are going to blind fold you both, and don't be afraid your Mother and I will hold your hands, while we do this, Nana and Papaw will carry your bags, Erin "what kind of crap is going on Mom"?

Sabrina pulled out from her pocket, and said "if you do this, two is your's and two are for Ben, now if you lollie gag to long, there going back into my pocket, do you understand!"

Ben smile "bring on the blindfolds, Erin "right on brother Ben!"

As they went back through the door, they walked into Gary Jr. house, Luke was in the basement, watching the T. V., when he heard voices up stairs, he came running up the stairs, "I was about to give up on you guys getting home, but when he saw his Mom and Dad with Nana, Papaw, Brent, Sabrina and Erin and Ben removing their blind folds, his Mom "we don't have time to explain, get a bag packed for a couple of day's!"

He was full of questions, "what's going on and why are you all here?"

Gary Jr. "do what your Mother said and do it now!" he was grumbling under his breath,!

Ben "hurry up you are going on an adventure, Papaw has invented a new way to travel!"

Gary Jr. brought something to blind fold Luke with, Luke saw Brent blind-folding Ben and then Erin!

He ask his Dad "what going on Pop?

Gary smiled at his sister, and pulled out 2 one hundred dollar bills, "son this is the way, I put this own, and you get these!"

Luke smiled "put it on Pop, and stuck the money in his pocket!"

Gary Jr. took him by the hand, and lead him through the door, with the rest And when they exited the Vault, they pulled the blindfolds off, all three of them, and all three of them wanted to know where they were?

Nana sat them down on her bed and told "them about Papa's, Great Uncle, Dyeing, and leaving him a great deal of money and this house, and a new way to travel!"

"and someday he will explain, but not now," she hugged each one of them, and "that their lives were about to change!"

"Your Mom's and Dad's are going to move here and live with us, I think you will find that you will love it to!"

"Now, I will let your parents take you and show where you will be living. now are there any questions? Ben "are we rich?" Nana smiled "I'll let your Mom tell you all about how well off you!"

Sabrina, she looked at Sabrina and Gary Jr. and said "I think you should show them where they'll be living," Sabrina "but Mom we'll have to convert the rooms for them to be comfortable here!"

Janice smiled "I know honey, but you have the resources to do just that!"

Gary Jr. "you know, I just realized, that we do, and that makes me feel good inside!"

As they all started leaving to go to there portion of the house, they came and hugged their parents, and "thanked them for being their Mom and Dad!"

The kids had already started exploring the house!

They were in Papa's game room, playing pool, when they were collected by their parents!

The den got quiet, Janice and Gary Pepper looked at each other, Janice "this isn't a dream is Pop?"

He took her into his arms and kissed her warmly, "honey if it's a dream, let's not wake up!"

When they did wake up it was two in the morning, they had cuddled on the couch and fallen asleep!

They had a very exhausting day, when Papa woke up he chuckled to himself, but with his wife's head laying on his chest, he felt a warmth he had never felt before, with the woman he loved!

He thought to himself, it just can't get any better than this!

He started kissing her on top of her head to get her to wake up, when she finally roused herself, she smiled, kissed him, and said "I guess we should go to bed now!"

When they woke up the next morning it was 8 thirty a.m., Janice chuckled, when she finally roused herself, she poked Gary Sr. and told him "it's time to get up, he sat up in bed, he looked around the room, then said, "it's all true!"

"We did inherit Uncle Pepper's money!"

Janice smiled at him then "I guess we did, because this isn't Stanley," Gary slid out from under the covers and sat on the side of the bed, Janice tossed him a robe, and said "the grandkids are in the game room playing, and you should have something to cover youself!"

"I guess your right, I wouldn't want to scare them to death, looking at this old body!"

Janice came around to him and slid her arms around him under his robe, "this body is as strong as 30 year old, and still has a lot of good times left in it!"

While she was rubbing up and down on his back and bottom, he laughed "young lady your turning me own," if you're not willing to pay off, you better back off!"

She smacked his bottom, and said "later old man!"

Janice went out on the porch, and he followed, they wanted to enjoy the morning air together, pulling two wicker chairs together, hold hands, just enjoying the sights and sounds!

Janice ask him "what he wanted to do today"?

Gary smiled "I would like to see, all of the property, and find out how Roland is managing the place!"

"And see if we should do something or leave it alone, from what I seen it all looks perfect!"

Janice "lets get some breadfast." "OK, then I want to talk to the boys!

And after that, maybe you girls would like to see all the property to! All 76 acers of it, you know it's a county, STONY KNOB, sounds impressive don't you think?"

They both found the way into the Kitchen, Sabrina, Brent, Sherry, Gary Jr. and Erin were eating breakfast!

Junior said "the boys are out looking the place over. Maria, greeted, them Janice told her, what they wanted, Maria smiled "that doesn't sound like a good breakfast, just let me give you something healthy," and she did, it wasn't to much, and they both enjoyed it!

CHAPTER 7

Gary Sr. ask "Maria, if Roland could take us on a tour of the property?"

Maria said "of coarse Mr. Pepper," she picked up the phone and called him Roland ask "what time they would like to go"?

Gary Sr. "what time, would be the most convient for him?"

Maria replied "would 10 o'clock be ok for you?"

Papa "sounds fine to me, tell him we'll see him at 10, in front of the house!"

Janice told "Maria, thank's for fixing breakfast for all of us, your going to spoil us, we usually have to fend for ourselves!"

Maria "Oh that's my job! and I love working in this state of the art kitchen, Mrs. Pepper, "you and I need to set down, and come up a menu, that would please you family!"

Janice "let me look over the property, and I'll get the girls together and see what we can come up with!"

When they all came out in the front of the house, Roland and Hector had two double seated golf carts for the tour, Roland said "I was surprised to see your Grandchildren, exploring the place this morning, we always check the gate at night!"

"That we didn't hear anyone leave the property last night. Mr. Pepper "we wanted to get them up here, it was late and we didn't want to disturb any of you!"

"My Son went for them, they will be here from now on, My two children and their family's, the house is big enough for all of us, and we already love the place!"

"Do you think that will be a burden on any of you folk's?"

Roland replied "no sir, we think that you and your, will be a blessing for us, it was a sad time, for the two years, the late Mr. Pepper was sick, and after he died, the place had a gloominess about it, then we found out from the Lawyers that you were coming, and the gloom about the place seemed to lift!"

"And we felt good you would be with us soon!"

Roland pulled up at the garage and got out, and said "if you will please follow me. I want to show you the two apartments above the garage, I saw the two young boy's out walking and looking this morning, I thought you might like to know about these apartments, Maria keeps them clean!"

When we got to stairs, at the end of the garage building, we all went up a flight of stairs, Roland unlocked the door, we all walked into a four room Apartment, fully furnished and beautifully decorated, Roland said "when Mr. and Mrs. Pepper were still healthy, they used these quarters for their guest, which they often had here at Stony Knob, they have all the amenities washers and dryers, and a large bathroom, with walkin closet!"

Gary Jr. smiled "when the ladies get mad at us, we'll have a real nice dog house to come to!"

Sherry slapped him on his back and said "I don't think so Buster, Roland led them to the other apartment and it was similar to the other one, Sabrina "we could put the boy's in one and Erin in the other, what do you think Papa?"

He laughed "sound like a plan to me, you wouldn't have to convert a room in your suite to accomadate them!"

Roland lead them back to the carts, and they stopped in front of his and Hector's quarters, they looked at both cottages, they were neet and clean, had all the amenities, they needed!

Gary Sr. ask Roland and Hector, if they needed anything?" Roland "explained that the late Mr. Pepper set up a budget for the County of Stony Knob, that takes care of all the needs here! If something breaks down, we have a group of contractors in Ashville and Weaverville that we call to take care of things we can't fix ourselves. All the systems that use water, sewer system, washing, bath waters, all these are recycled and used for the grounds, flowers!"

"Mr. Pepper, won an award from the State for his conservation efforts, during the drought the State was having, we didn't have any water problems during that period, and Mr. Pepper was very pleased about that!"

As Roland drove them around the property, he explained why there was a chain link fence all around the property, "at that time there were bears getting to close to the houses, and he thought that would stop them, and it did, we check the fince once a month to make sure it's still in good condition, and that no trees have fallen on it!"

As they were ending their tour of the property, they all thought the view's were beautiful from every vantage point on the property!

As they pulled up in front of the house, and got out of the carts, Roland "I need to talk to you Mr. Pepper," Gary Sr. turned and back to the cart, Roland said "a man came by a week after the late Mr. Pepper died, showing a badge and said he was from the Government and wanted to search the house, Hector and I are Deputy Sheriffs, under the Sheriff, which is you now, we wouldn't let him on the property, he didn't push us to let him through the gate, but he did leave a card, said he would return and talk to you!" Roland ask "him to come with him!"

Gary Sr. ask "Gray Jr. and Brent, to come along with them!"

Roland drove them to the end of the garage, got out pulled up a garage door and under it was another door. He got out some keys, opened it, Gary Sr. ask "what is this?"

Roland, told him "this is the County office of Stony Knob!"

They all walked into the office, there was a long board room table with six large leather chairs on casters around the table!

When Brent saw how nice the office was, he said "wow this is a nice office.

Gary Jr. "what all this about Pop?"

Gary Sr. "I don't know son, but Roland and Hector will explain it now!"

He set them down around the table and started asking questions!

Roland started explaining, in order to become a county, there were requirement's, we had to have a County Sheriff, which is you!"

"We are deputy sheriff's, now that you have a son and a son in law, you can deputize them!"

Brent said "do we have to carry gun's!" Roland smiled "we do have them, but so far we haven't needed to carry them!"

"But after the man came to search the property!" We've kept them close, because we didn't know what he'd do!"

Roland got up and went to the desk, picked up the card and gave it to Mr. Pepper and said "I thought it was strange that the FBI would want to search the house, because Mr. Pepper was a quiet and honest man."

"He was always forthright, with us since we came to this country. The only one we could trust, he was always fair, never mean, and never tried to cheat us!

At first he was a very strict task master, but after his wife died, he became lonely and would eat with us!"

"I think he grew to love us. as much as we came to love him, the children called him Patron, he was their Godfather!"

He found the Deptuy badges, and gave one to Gary Jr. and one to Brent, he reached back into the bag and pulled out two holstered guns and said "these are loaded," as he removed them from the holsters, and dropped the clip's out and gave Gary Jr. a gun, the loose clip, then he gave Brent one

Brent's eyes got big as saucers, when Gary Jr. saw the reaction of Brent he laughed out loud, as well as everyone at the table did!

Gary Sr. "don't worry Brent, we'll keep the guns away from the kids," then he got up from the table, shook, Roland and Hector and told them "If there's anything from us, just let all three of us know! and we'll take care of it, or find someone who can!"

Roland and Hector left!

He looked at Brent and Gary Jr., "I think the cat just got out the bag, about Merlin's door!"

Wade Hound

Wade Hound was setting at his desk, in Washington D.C. somewhere in the Hover building, looking over all the information he had received from the CIA about what sounded like a lot of crap to him!"

Wade had been with the Bureau for 15 years, and thought who wanted to shaft him with this Job, he picked up the phone and called Leonard his section Chief, "what the hell are you trying to do to me, with this kind of crap?"

Leonard laughed, and said, "slow down and come over to my office, and I'll try to explain it to you!"

When he got to Leonard's office, he was still fuming. He sat down in front of Leonard Walleye's desk, and thought to himself what kind of name is that?

Then laughed "Walleye, what do you want from me?" Well Hound Dog, the man upstairs said to put the best man on this job, to sniff out this story!

What you were not told, was this crap, was in a stash of information the Germans were compiling, at the end of world war 2, I think you knew that Hitler was into the occults, he was trying to find an easy way to take over the World!"

"This new information came from the bunker in Berlin, some kids found a stash of papers, and were trying to sell them!"

"The CIA found out about them, and snatched them, and passed them on to their organization, it seemed to their experts, that Merlin and Arthur did live and die, that Merlin, had left behind a magical door, they traced it back to an Antique Shop in London!"

"It seems that the shop had been in one family, for generation's, the owner found records of a Mrs. Pepper, buying an antique door and shipped it back to North Carolina, to a place called Stony Knob!"

Wade chuckled, then said "just what do you want me to do about it, if Mrs. So and So did buy an antique door, the door belongs to her!"

Lenoard said, "the man up stairs wants his Hound dog to check and see if there's any truth to the Story!"

"He knows that if you check into it, that you will find out everything you can!"

"There're giving you all the time you need," Leonard "Wade, just think of it as a paid Vacation!"

"And who wouldn't want to go to the beautiful mountains of North Carolina it's cool at night, and I think it will improve your attitude, maybe even put a spring in your step, and it might even improve your complexion!"

Wade laughed at that as he stood up and said "well Leonard, this dude is off to Ashville, North Carolina!"

"And it sounds like I have a blank check on this one!"

Leonard, said "you do, and take care of yourself," a company plane flew him down to Ashville N. C.!

While he was in the air, on his way, he had fallen asleep and was dreaming of his wife, who had died!

Almost two years ago, he had loved her almost all of his life, their family's had lived next door to each other, she was born one day before he was, they had played together all their lives, and as long as he could remember he loved her, they were sweethearts in grammer school, and had continued dating in High School and all through collage!

They lived together all through the University years, he tried hard not to get her pregnant! their parents would have been very disappointed in them both. his parents had warned him if he got her pregnant, he would have to quit school and support her and the baby!

But nothing happened and they enjoyed themselves together, after they finished School they got married! they wanted to start a family, right away, he was hired by the Federal Government, working for the FBI, their parents had bought a condo for them in Washington D. C., she had been hired as a Law Clerk at the Supreme Court!

CHAPTER 8

They tried very hard, to get her pregnant, they were doing it like Monkeys and enjoying it!

So after a year, she decided to seek help!

That's when the Doctor found the cancer, she lived for two more year's, and was gone, leaving him all alone!

And for a year, he wanted to join her, until he sought counseling, at the psychology Dept. of the FBI!

It was there that he fealized he had to go on living, for both of them!

That he had her for most of his life!

He would tuck her into his heart, and carry her there always!

He had his Mom and Dad, and her folks to come to D.C to clean out her cloths and other personal things!

He then poured himself into his work and soon became known as the Hound Dog, if there was a problem, he could solve it, and he had a reputation for solving every case that was give to him, and helping others to solve theirs

As they were landing in Ashville N. C. he roused and thought its been 16 years, that he could retire at 20 years, he knew he could retire in 4 more years!

He thanked the pilots, as he got off the plane, there was a car, and a man standing beside it, as he got closer to the car he recognized the man, stand-ing, waiting for him, he put his hand out, and said Damn, "Jack Short, it sure is good to see a face I know!"

"Wade you are looking good for an old man!"

Wade smiled then said, Jack old buddy, you're ahead of me, and by a few years!"

As they got into the car, Jack was asking "what the hell are you doing here in the South!"

Wade said "you mean nobody told the office what I would be doing here?"

Jack "not a word, except to help you any way we could, and that came from the Director of the FBI, the big boy himself!"

Jack "its lunch time, where do you want to go eat!"

Wade smiled "Jack this is your town, I've never been here before, you'll have to take me somewhere that don't serve heart burn!"

Jack said "I'd forgotton you'd never been South before. You're in for a treat, most of the time this is a quiet and pleasant place to live and work.

We've made reservations for a suite at the Grove Park Inn for you, they Serve very good food, and you can check in, and we can eat there. Smitty is getting you a car, its probably already there!"

As they were driving into the Inn, Wade was admiring, the beautiful Mountain scenery, and told "Jack, I think I'll enjoy staying in this part of country, who knows, I might just want to stay longer than they want me to!"

Jack laughed and said "that sounds encouraging!"

Wade told "Jack I don't want anyone knowing, I'm with the FBI not just yet, if any questions are ask at the Hotel, tell them I'm a businessman! I will flash the badge when I need to!"

Jack "that's fine with me Buddy!"

As they pulled into the Grove Park Inn, Jack gave the keys to the Parking attendant and he pulled the luggage from the trunk, and gave them to the bellboy!

Wade and Jack went into the Hotel, as Wade was checking in the clerk ask "sir how long will you be staying, Wade "it could be just a couple of weeks, but it could be longer, I'll let you know!"

The clerk "that will be fine sir," after the clerk gave him his key card, Jack "what's for lunch today?" The Clerk gave him a menu "have a good day,

We hope you enjoy your stay sir!" As they were eating, Jack was telling Wade, all about his children, and Wade was enjoying hearing Jack talking about them!

He thought, if only we could have had children, I would still have a part of his wife around!

Then he roused himself out of that train of thought! Jack noticed he was talking to himself, "Wade I'm sorry for boring you with the family!"

Wade looked at Jack then said "no no, your not boring me, it was fun hearing about a normal family life!"

Jack ask "are you going back with me to the office!" Wade replied "no I I'll just check in with you if I need any help!" then Jack "well maybe you could come for dinner at the house and meet the wife and kids!"

Wade 'that sounds good to me!"

Jack left for the office, Wade went to his room feeling a little grungy, so he took a shower!

After that he felt refreshed, he had already stored his gear, he sat down and opened his brief, took out the information on where the Peppers lived! it was still early in the day, so he decided to take a drive to see if he could find the place called Stony Knob, he went downstairs and picked up the car key's they had left for him!

Wade loaded the information into the pathfinder, the directions took him through some of the most beautiful mountain scenery, he thought he had evey seen!

He had been driving for about an hour, when he pulled into a private drive that said Stony Knob!

When he reached the gate, he got out of his car and pushed the call button Roland answered, Wade introduced himself "as an FBI agent and wanted to talk to Mr. George Pepper!

Roland "I'll be come down to the gate." Five minutes later he walked through a side door of the gate with Hector. They all shook hands, Wade said "I wanted to talk with Mr. George Pepper!

Hector replied "Mr. Pepper died last week! Could we help you?"

Wade "well I wanted to look his home, he pulled out a badge and let them both see it!

Roland "I'm sorry but we can't let you do that. Mr. Pepper has relatives But they haven't been notified yet, they will be notified three weeks after his death!

"Wade so you wouldn't let me look around in the house?"

Hector "no sir, you'll have to wait until the new owners arrive, they might let you look, but we can't do it!"

Roland "would mind telling us what this is all about?"

Wade "I'm not at liberty to discuss that with you!"

He got back into his car, and drove back to Ashville, enjoying the beautiful sights of the Mountains!

Then he thought about Jack, and his offer to eat Dinner with his Family, so he called Jack on his cell phone!

When Jack answered, Wade ask "if the Dinner invitation was still open,"

Jack replied "of coarse, we would love to have you, I was just walking out the door, on my way home!"

Jack gave him his address, Wade quickly entered the address into his path-finder, and said "see you at 5 thirty, I'm just 20 minutes away!"

Jack hung up, Wade was right behind him, as they pulled into Jacks drive way. They walked into the house together, when Jack opened the door a young lady about 10 years old, came running up to Jack and was hugging his neck, and kissing him, she was glad he was home!

She said "Mom got a pot roast for supper, your favorite dish!"

Jack stopped her, and introduced, this is Wade Hound, and Wade this is Ginger, our baby girl, Ginger giggled "Hound dog!"

Wade chuckled, you've got that right young lady." Wade thought she was a fine looking young Lady!

And Wade ask her "for a hugg," she hugged him and said "lets go get some-thing to eat, I'm starving!"

She lead them both into the dinning room, Susan was putting the food on the table, when they got there!

Susan hugged Jack, "Wade Hound it's been a very long time since. I've seen you." When Jack called and said you were coming for Dinner, "I couldn't remember you, but now that I've seen you, how could I not remember you, a very fun guy to be around!"

"Now you set there and pointed to a place at the table!"

Jack you'll have to get the boy's, I've already called them twice!" "Yes love there both knuckle heads, He motioned for Wade to come with him, they went out to the back of the house, there were two young boy's, horsing around in a pool, when they saw there Father, Roger the oldest, "Sorry Dad, the time just got lost!"

Jack looked at his watch, "you've got five minutes, to get dry and dressed and at the table!"

"Your Mother said she called you twice, and if you're not at the table in five minutes. There could be some grounding for both of you guys, do you under stand?"

They both dropped their trunks and were running to the changing room, with towels flying!"

As Jack and Wade went back into the house, Jack started laughting and said "those two are a lot of fun to be around, they remind me, so much of me, when I was that age!"

"Watch them, it'll take them less than two minutes to get to the table!"

And apologize to their Mother!"

When Jack and Wade sat down, the younger boy told "his Mother, they were sorry for being late!"

Jack introduced them to his friend from the Bureau, the boy's looked at him and smiled. Wade held up his hand and said, "your sister has already inquired about Hound dog!"

Jack smiled "this Hound dog has solved more cases, than anyone else at the Bureau!"

Wade smiled "yes I have, because I've had more time to look at cases, and I've helped a few others solve their's to!"

But this is not the office, and I want to hear about how you guys are doing!"

Wade was looking at the children, when he said it!

And they were eager to talk to him, about there lives, and they talked for a good 30 minutes!

Until a very attractive young girl, walked into the dinning room, Roger looked at his Father and said "may I be excused from the table!"

Jack said "you may go, but be in bed by 11 o'clock young man!" Roger "yes Sir!"

As they started to leave he introduced her to Wade. "This is my best friend Stephanie, and this is Wade Hound, he's a friend of Dad's they work together!"

She came over and shook his hand and said "very pleased to meet you sir!"

Wade smiled and said "nice to meet you too." And they left the room, the other two children, ask to leave the table, and they were gone!

Wade smiled "how do you handle the love birds, Susan smiled "we have to watch them close, she is our next door neighbor daughter, she and Roger been companions all their lives, and they are together all the time. and we know they love each other a lot, but we've made it clear to them, that they must get through school first!"

Jack "Roger came to me when he was 12 years old and ask if he could marry Stephanie!"

And that shocked us, and they are together much as we let them be, I feel like she's our child!"

"Jack we saw them to gether having sex, so I gave him the protection he needs, her Mom put her on the pill, and I told him if she gets pregnant he he will have to take care of the child and her!"

"However I couldn't put my child through that!"

CHAPTER 9

W ade "I know how you feel, our parents were good friends and next door neighbors. I always knew I loved my wife, and that we would spend the rest of our lives together, but as you know, when we graduated from school together, and got married and were looking forward to having a house full of kids!"

"But as you know it wasn't to be, she died three years after we were married!"

"I love that you have children, take care of them, because they grow so fast, even faster than you think!"

Susan smiled "it seems like they were born just yesterday, now they think there grown, and they getting more independent as they grow older, which is what we want them to be!"

Wade was enjoying talking to Jack and Susan about their children!

In Washington he had a set routine, work, eat and sleep, he loved what he did, but at times it was also boring, and just to have someone to talk to was comforting!

He looked at his watch, "Holy Cow! its 10 thirty, I've let the time get away from me! He looked at Jack and Susan, I am sorry I didn't mean to stay this long and bother you guy's!"

Jack said "it's been fun talking to you Wade, I could tell you needed the time with another human being, I know when I'm away from Susan and the Kids, I get very lonely to!" Do you know how long you will be here?"

Wade "I was thinking I could rap this all up in a couple of days, but now the people I have to talk to!"

"And now it look's like 3 or 4 weeks, before I will be able to talk to them!"

So I'm going to enjoy myself, and see some of this lovely country!"

And hope to pester you folks, until you put a sign in the front yard, saying you've moved and left no forwarding address! Then I'll know that I've warn out my welcome!

"And Susan you are an excellent cook, and hope to be invited back again for supper!"

Wade "I know, why not let me take you and your family out to eat tomorrow night?"

Susan "now that sounds fine to me," Wade "you'll have to pick a place?"

"Jack and I ate lunch at the Grove Park Inn, and it was pretty good, but you must decide where we eat?"

It was almost 11 before Wade, walked out of their house, as he was leaving he ask "Jack if Roger was in bed yet," Jack replied "yes, I saw him sneaking in just 5 minutes ago, he knows I love him very much, but that I want cut him much slack in the romance department, we know they'll get married and have a house full of kids, someday!

"But they both know, there is a lot of schooling before they can marry! they're both smart kids!"

As Wade was walking into his suite, at the Grove Park Inn, he was thinking how good it felt, to be away from Washington D. C., he was thinking maybe it was time for him to leave his job!

But the next morning, the Job was all he knew, he might like to be stationed in a place like this with a low-key job, pushing papet around for a few days a week!

He shaved, showered, and went down for breakfast, as he was eating, he was browsing through the local paper, there was an article, that got his attention, that there was an heir to the Pepper fortune, the Law firm handling the Estate said that the will stipulated that the heir, not be notified for three weeks after his death!

Wade took another sip of his coffee and that's strange. He'd check out the Law firm handling the Estate!

So for the next week and a half, he did just that. When he finished, he had discovered that George Pepper had founded the firm, and the only reason he had delayed notifying the next of kin, was that he didn't know he had any!

Until a few weeks before he died! Then Wade found out that Stony Knob was a county, in the State of North Carolina, he fully researched how and why George Pepper had done that!

It was all legal, and that Mr. Pepper, was a very smart man, the legal work was a brilliant piece of Law!

He looked at his taxes, but couldn't anything wrong. He had always over paid his taxes!

George Pepper was an honest man!

Wade got Jack to post a man, close to Stony Knob, to let him know when the new owner took possession of the property!

He checked the new owners out. When he finely got the name of the heir, a Gary Norman Pepper, he had a wife, and two grown children, and three grandchildren!

He ran him through the system. He couldn't find anything wrong with their back ground!

Other than he was one hell of lucky guy. Wade fell in love with this part of the country, and he started looking for some realestate. With the help of Jack and Susan!

He was about to close on a piece of property that Susan loved, and the kids wanted him to buy!

It was an older home with 8 room that had been refurbished with killer decks, that set on top of a mountain with a swimming pool, and a tennis coart!

With Wade life style since his wife died, he could afford it. He sold his D.C. apartment for the same price he was paying for the house, 900,000 thousand the house was completely furnished and decorated!

Jack and Susan and the kids, had adopted Wade and called him Uncle Hound Dog!

And he loved them, and the oldest Boy and his girl friend, Stephanie, reminded him of him and his wife, when they were growing up, he felt for them!

When he moved out of the Grove Park Inn and into his new home, he gave Roger a key to the house and told him that he and Stephanie could use the place, when they needed to, but it would not be wise to tell his Mom and Dad, that they would chew us both out about it, and he reminded him of how much he loved their whole family!

Wade checked his calender, it had been four weeks since the death of Mr. Pepper!

Jack told him that the man watching the house at Stony Knob, had told him that the new owners were settled in and that everything was looking normal, that nothing unusual was happening!

Wade thought it was time to visit Stony Knob, so he headed toward Weaverville. He was still amazed at how beautiful the Mountains were he decided to call the Pepper's on his way, he got Janice on the phone, "he introduced himself, and ask if he could talk to Gary Pepper," in a few minutes, Gary answered the phone and ask "who was calling?" Wade introduced himself again, and told" him he was on his way visit him." Gary ask "do I know you?"

He said "no sir you don't, I left a calling card with a Mr. Roland some time ago," Gary replied "oh yes, he told me the second day after we arrived, and he gave me your card!"

Then Gary told him to hold on a miunte, when he got the card, he picked up the phone and said, "FBI Wade, do I need a Lawyer when I talk to you?"

Wade "no sir I don't think that's needed, I would like to talk to you about something your Great Aunt purchased in England, and by the way I'm at your gate now!"

Gary "let me open the gate for you, come up to the main house, I'll be waiting for you there!"

While Wade was driving up to the house, Gary told Janice "to get the boy's there PDQ," As he was opening the front door and stepping out, Wade was stopping in front of the house, he was out of the car and up to the door.

Gary and Wade shook hands, Wade showed him his I.D. and said could we go inside. If I remember correctly Roland said "you wanted to search my home!

And I don't think you have the right to do that!, That's why I asked if I need a Lawyer!"

You told me that I didn't need one, Wade "I'm sorry if I left the impression that I wanted to search your home!"

"I'm on a fact finding mission for the Government," he went back to the car got a brief case, Gary looked at Wade and ask, would you like something to drink, nothing hard of coarse, a soft drink, or a beer! I think one of the boy's might have a beer, I don't care much for beer myself, sometimes a glass of Wine, but mostly I like a soft drink!" Wade responded, I sure would like a soft drink, I had country ham for breakfast this morning, and it always makes thirsty!

Gary "come on in Wade, we'll find you something," he showed him into the den, have a seat, and "I'll get Maria to bring us something cold to drink."

As he started looking for Maria, Brent walked into the den, Gary introduced him to Wade "this is my son-in-law, Brent Messer, and Gary Jr. came in with his Mother, Gary Sr., "Wade this my wife, Janice, and the handsome guy is my son Gary Jr." Wade responded to all of them, with "it's good to meet you!

Gary said "honey I'm getting us something cold to drink, would you like something?"

Janice responded with "that would be nice, Gary Jr. said "Pop I would like a coke, if you don't mind." He looked at Wade do you have a preference for a soft drink!

Wake smiled a coke will do fine. Just then Maria came into the room, and ask if anyone wanded anything to drink, Gary Sr. smiled and said, "I would like a coke to! I was on my way, to get soft drinks for us all!"

Maria would you mind doing that for us, she replied "not at all, would you want them in a glass with ice or in the bottle's?

The drinks are already cold, Gary Sr. looked at Wade, "what would you prefer?" In the bottle would be fine!"

Thay sat down, Gary Sr. gave the folder to Janice, when she read it, she gave the folder to Gary Jr. after he read it, he gave to Brent. Janice looked at Wade, and said "what do you want from us Mr. Hound!"

Wade "well after I first read the report from the CIA, I thought they were all crazy." But the Director of the FBI, wanted me to investigate and find out if it's true!"

"From all indecation the story was true. Hitler had tried to find the door and followed its path to England, this all happened just at the end of WW11, our own Government followed that same path to an antique shop in London England!"

And there a Mrs. Pepper bought it and shipped it home to Stony Knob North Carolina," Wade "what I would like to know is if you folks know any-thing about a Magical door?"

Wade smiled "it still sounds like hog wash to me, but the Director want to find out if it's here, and what it dose!"

"After I arrived here, I fell in love with this part of the country. I just bought a home here in Ashville and I think I'll stay in this part of the country for the rest of life, I love it that much!"

The he looked at Gary Sr. "all I want to know is, if you know anything about the door, that was shipped here?" I know you haven't been here but a week, Gary Sr. looked at his family and said, "what do you guys think about about what he's telling us!"

"You have as much imput here as I do. What I'm trying to say is, should we tell him about what we know!"

Gary Jr. "well Pop, it might not be a bad idea to let the Government know, if they've found out about it, there might be others who have found out to, I don't think some people on this planet, would ask, they'd just take it.

Just then Sabrina ans Sherry walked into the room with packages. They had been shopping!

CHAPTER 10

"What are you guys doing, all clustered together?" Then she saw Wade and "introduced herself, then to Sherry, adding, I'm the Daughter, Sherry is the Daughter in law, Gary Jr. Wife, and you are?" Wade stood up, taking out his ID's and handing them to her!

She smiled and said, "as in hound dog?" "That's what they call me at the shop!"

Sabrina ask if I could check on you I.D. at the FBI offices in Washington?"

Wade "of coarse not!"

Sabrina took his I.D. and said "I be right back, as soon as I can confirm that you are, who you, say you are, Mr. Hound!"

Sabrina and Janice left the room, Wade telling Gary Sr. how beautiful their place was, then he started telling them about his Home, how it was on top of a Mountain, with some beautiful views, from his decks, and how thrilled he was being able to buy it!"

"That he would stay here, even if the Bureau, told him he couldn't, that he would be forced to retire, if it came to that!"

Brent ask "how long he had been with the FBI?" Wade replied "16 years, I only have 4 more years, until I can retire with full benefits. But if I have to back to the Washington grind, I would just retire now!" Sabrina and Janice came back into the room, with a piece of paper off the fax Machine and passed it around to the family!

They all looked at it, then passed it over to Wade, it was a photo of him with all the pertinent information about him. It was from the Director of the FBI Wade smiled and said "they seemed to like me up there, I get thing done for them!

Gary Sr. "Wade, I'm going to take the family out into the Foyer and have a discussion with them, and we'll let you know what we are willing to do in this matter!"

They gathered in Sabrina portion of the house, so Wade couldn't hear them.

Gary Jr. "if those guys found it, who else will come along and take it from us!"

Brent "how will they know where to find it," Sabrina the Bad people can fill you with drugs and find out anything they want to know."

Janice looked at her Husband, "what do you want to do about it?" He said

"I've always thought of my self as an honest man and we do have the door, it was willed to me, so it belong to us, are we willing to fight for it?"

Janice "honey you and I are not able to fight for anything, and were not having a gun fight at the OK corel, I have children and grandchildren to think about!"

Papa smiled and said "we could hire an Army," he laughed "I was only kidding," and they all laughed at that!

He "all kidding aside, lets take a vote on it, what ever we decide, we'll do!"

And if they decide, they got to have it. we'll consider selling it," they all they all woted to expose the door to Wade with caution!

They all went back to the den, with Wade, Gary Sr. brought with him the brief that had been given to him at the reading of the will, Gary Sr. said "Wade there is a door, that was created by Merlin, the Magician, in the house!"

Gary Sr. "would you mind explaining to me why the Government of the Unite States would want to know about it?"

When Wade finished reading the folder, he said "Holy Cow!!" "So there was something to all that information! That's hard to belive, shaking his head, he said "Holy Moly" "can I see it now?"

Gary Sr. said, "I have a Vault that I don't want you know where it is!"

"Gary Jr., Brent and I will get it and bring it here!"

And they were back within 5 minutes, Gary Sr. "I thought it would be heavy to move, but the chaps got it out of the Vault in no time!"

They parked it, next to an end table in the den, turning it toward Wade, who jumped up as they came into the room, and was admiring the craft-manship of the carving on the door!

Wade said "that is so well done!" he started to touch it, Gary Sr. "Wade I don't want your finger prints on my door! you can look, but don't touch it please!"

Wade "sorry, I just thought it was so beautifully done. What dose it do ?"

Gary Sr. ask "where would you like to go, Mr. Hound, dog? Would you like to go to Washington, Paris France, or London England?"

Wade look at him funny, "what are you saying, that you can go to all of those through that door!"

Gary Sr. smiled "Wade it magic, and I guess anything is possible!"

Wade said "I would like to go to my Office in the Hover Building, in Washington D.C.!"

Gary Sr. smiled, "Wade I don't know where the office is, so if you will hold my hand and think of where in the building, you want to be!"

Gary opened the door and they stepped into Wade office, Wade said (damn, damn) "this is not possible!"

Gary ask "is this the right office?" Wade walked around the desk, picked up his name plate, and showed it, Gary read the plate Wade Hound, and under the name was inscribed (Hound Dog)!

Wade picked up the phone and called Leonard, when he answered, Wade "Walleye come into my office now!"

And in a few minutes a man walked into Wade's office, he looked surprised how the hell did you get by me, and who is this man with you?"

"Leonard sit down!" Wade said "This is the Magic man, Mr. Gary Pepper Sr.

"Remember that little job you gave me!"

Leonard "I didn't give you that job, the Director of the FBI gave you that Job!"

"What the hell are you doing back in Washington?" Wade turned to Gary and said "this is going to blow their minds!"

Wade ask "is the Director in his office?" Leonard replied "sure, I just left him a few minutes ago. Well I think you better get him down here! We have some very interesting new's for the FBI I think it will change a lot of things around here, and for a lot of people!"

Leonard picked up the phone, then said "guess who's here in his office? You should get down here and take a look!"

Lenoard said "now would you tell me what your doing here!? Wade "lets just wait for the coach to get here!"

The Director of the FBI was in Wade office with in 5 minutes, when he entered! Wade "Gary this is the Director of the FBI Sandy Lowe, and Sandy this is Gary Pepper Sr., they shook hands!

Wade ask "them if they saw anything strange or different, in this room,"

Sandy and Leonard both looked at him strangly, and said "no," Wade said "believe it or not there's a door that Merlin the

Magician, conjured up, and it's in this room, none of us can see it, except Mr. Pepper, Gary would you take us to your fine home!"

Gary smiled "lets go," he opened the door and he and Wade walked into his home, Leonard and Sandy seemed to be slow in responding, by what they just saw, and didn't move until Gary motioned for them to come in!

But when they got inside of his house, it took them a few minutes, to belive that they had just left Washington, and were in North Carolina!

When the kids started talking to their Father, he stopped them and "introduced them to the Director of the FBI, this is Mr. Lowe and Mr. Walleye!"

And each one shook their hands, and introduced themselves, to both men!

Sandy I need to set down for a moment to take this all in, Leonard did the same!

After a moment, he look at Wade "do you realize what this means! We have to tell the President!"

Wade "don't you think we should talk to Mr. Pepper, he own's the door!"

Sandy "this is overwhelming!"

"I think we should talk to the President!" Wade "I have my cell phone," then Wade looked at Sandy and he could see the wheels turning, in his eyes,

Sandy! Come back to earth, what are you thinking, Sandy smiled "it's still overwhelming!"

"Let me call the President, and warn him we're coming, we don't want to be shot by the Secret Service! When we suddenly appear!"

He took Wade's phone and dialed the President's office and ask to speak to when he answered, this is Saney, "Andrew, are you in your office? Are you alone?" The President said "Sandy you are sounding very strange, what with you!" Well Andrew it is it's something very, strange and I'm about to show you, right now!"

The President "Sandy you know my office is always open to you!" Sandy "I know that sir, but well'll be there rather fast and I don't want to be shot by your troops in doing so!"

Andrew "Sandy you're sounding even more strange the more you talk!"

Sandy "well sir we'll see you soon!"

And he hung up the Phone, gave it back to Wade, Sandy looked at Gary "would please, take us to the White House, to the President Ovel office!"

Gary "I think we could do that, but could I take my children? we've never met the President!"

Sandy smiled "well Mr. Pepper, I think we should wait until later for that, this is going to be a big enough shock, when we just pop into the President's Oval Office as it is!"

Gary "I do understand, are we ready to go?"

Wade, Leonard and Sandy stood up and walked over to the door. As Gary, started to open the door, he look at his wife, "come on Love, if these guy's don't like it, they can just walk home, and that's a powerful long walk!"

Janice got up and took his hand as he opened the door into the Oval office.

The President stood up very quickly as five people stepped into the room from the wall!

He looked at all five People, and said "how the hell did you do that?"

Sandy "this is the reason, I sounded so strange, when I talked to you a few minutes ago! You remember the door, you had me put Wade (the hound Hound dog) on to looking for, well sir he found it!"

And this is Mr. & Mrs. Pepper," they walked over and shook his hand, Janice, sir you had our vote, last election, Gary "we like the way you're running our Country sir! and hope you can stay for awhile!

Andrew smiled "well thank you, that sounds good to me!"

Then the President "would you excuse me, I have to sit down for a few a few minutes. Ane he invited them all to have a seat!"

He looked at them all, "you do know this is impossible!" Gary replied I know what you mean, but we just came from North Carolina!"

The President looked at his watch, and said is any one else as hungry as I am?

Janice looked Papa, "sorry honey, I was so excited about coming with you that I forgot about dinner!"

Janice looked at the others, Gary's a diabetic," the President "we could get him something to eat, and I'm starving to!"

"what would you like to eat Gary?"

Gary smiled "well if I remember correctly, Maria was getting ready for supper just before we came here! "Sir how would you like go to the old North State, and you could be back in notime!"

The President looked at Sandy, "what would it take to go with them!"

Sandy "I don't want to go there," he looked at Gary "the President has an army of secret service people that would have a fit, if he were gone, for thirty minutes. I don't think we should do that sir!"

Gary smiled "sir I wish you could come with us, but I understand if you can't, but I've got to eat!"

CHAPTER 11

"Now Wade has a car parked in front of my house, so I know he has to come back with me, but you guy's, your back in Washington it would be best if called a cab or maybe the President would give you a ride! Gary laughed, "sorry about that Mr. President, I just couldn't resist saying that, it sounded funny to me!"

Janice slapped his arm "Papa you know better than to say that in front of the President of the United State's of America!"

They all laughed at that. Sandy "Andrew, I think you need to try this to see how amazing it is!

Gary "sir you could go through and turn around and come back, before any-one knows you gone!"

Andrew looked at Sandy "would we do that?"

Sandy "yes sir, and if you want, you could take some of you guards! But I don't think there need, the Pepper family are just good American's, and you have the best 3 FBI guy's there is sir!

Andrew "I've just go to see this thing in action!" he turned to Sandy "lead the way!" Sandy smiled, Sir you'll have to follow the Pepper's, there the only people that can see the door, that leads out of your office!" Gary "we don't know why, but my wife and I are the only one's, that can see it here at the end of our destination, even our children can't see it eather, so I know none of you can see it! Andrew, went to the wall they all came out of, he felt all around the wall, "I can't see or feel anything unusual, but I know this is where you guys came out of the wall!"

Janice walked over and opened the door, and they all went into the den of the Pepper home!

The President, this is hard to belive. He walked over to the windows and "wow that is a beautiful view!" It was getting dusty bark out side and the lights of Weaverville were on. Gary walked over to him, smiled "this is Paradise, maybe some day you could come for a visit and stay for a while, now that you here, you've got to meet my family!"

He turned to tell Janice to go get the kids, but she was gone, "Wade would you follow the noise into the game room, and tell my children to come meet the President of the United States!"

Wade was ushering the crowed out of the game room, and Gary "introduced them all including his grandchildren!"

The President smiled "they're a fine group of voters!"

He looked at his watch, "we've been gone for 10 minutes, we had better get back to mind the store!"

He smiled as he said this, "Gary we'll have a long talk about what you've here, I'll get Sandy to set up a meeting with you very soon, maybe, tomorrow!"

And he went to the door, "he said I can see it here and opened the it, then he said what the hell!"

Gary "sir please close the door, and he did, that's one of the things we don't understand yet. My wife and I are the only people that can use it, my children can't use it, unless Janice or I activate it, so we not let them mess with it!"

"We keep it in a Vault, I want tell anyone where it is for our own safty!"

Gary opened the door into the Oval Office, and the President, Sandy and Leonard walked into the Oval Office!

Andrew Mellon the President said "Gary you have a good night!" Gary "same to you Sir!"

Janice came into the den "alright old man, lets get something to eat."

She looked at Wade "you should eat something to." The 3 of them went into the kitchen, there were roast beef sandwiches, already prepared!

Wade took a bit "this sure hit's the spot!" Gary "I know what you mean, I was getting hungry to, Honey who fixed the roast beef?" Janice replied,

"Papa you know who did them, Maria of coarse!"

Wade smiled "I wonder if I could steal away from you guys." Janice "she comes with a package, a husband and 2 good size boy's!"

Wade "with my new home in Ashville, you guys will have to come to see me!"

Gary "that sounds good to me, we don't actually know a lot of people in this neck of the woods, Wade I think we are going to be good friends!"

Wade smiled "I would like that, I'm new in this area to!" after eating, they sat and talked about the door, Wade "I think you should keep this a secret. If anyone else finds out what you've got here, they'll come after it, Gary smiled "Wade that's what we were doing, before you came looking for it!"

Wade "its still hard for me to belive, what that thing can do. Just think of the security the President would have, if he had control of it. No more Air Force one, no need for it!"

Gary smiled "I hadn't thought about that, all I wanted to do was go to Las Vegas and places like that for fun!

My Great Uncle and Aunt, used it to go to dinner all over the World, they also liked to play slot machines, My Aunt loved to go to Monty Carlo to play there!"

The note he left me, warned me about telling anyone about the door. But I felt I could trust you Wade!"

Wade "I always had the ability to read people, and I sensed you were a trust worthy person!"

Wade "gosh its 11 o'clock, I had better, hit the road." Janice "you could spend the night here, we have 2 apartments over the Garage, If you don't want to drive this late!"

Wade "I can tell you don't mind." Janice smiled "of coarse not, please do!"

Janice got the keys for him, Gary ask "if she had turned on the porch lights over there for him!"

Janice "Wade there are towels and even shaving gear for you over there!"

She smiled "and No you can't have Maria!"

Wade Laughed and they walked him out to his car, Janice if there anything just give us a buzz!"

"Maria is usually in the kitchen at 7 thirty!" they watched him pull his car over to the apartment and climb the stairs, Gary got the door from the den and put it back into the Vault. And they went to bed. they were both tired!

When they woke up the next morning, the Vault door was standing wide open!

Gary got up and looked inside, Merlin's door was gone, He started to panic.

Someone had been in their bedroom, while they were sleeping! they had not know they were there. He picked up the phone and called Wade in the guest house!

He thought to him self, Wade was the culprit in this, the phone rang 6 or 7 times, just when he started to hang up!

Wade answered the phone, Gary ask "If he had a good rest?" Wade "I sure did, I didn't want to get up, I didn't fully wake up until I got into the shower."

Gary "so that's why you didn't answer the phone?"

Wade "yes! Gary said "I've got some bad news, when we woke up this morning the Vault was open, and Merlin's door is gone!

Do you know anything about this?"

Wade "hell no, he said don't touch a thing and I'll be right over there!"

Wade was there within 3 minutes. "The Hound dog was there," he had a he had a black light with him, he scoped all around the Vault door, I can't any evidence that the Vault door has been forced open!

"Is everyone here in the house ok? Janice looked at Gary "I didn't think about the kids. Oh, I hope there all alright!"

She picked up the phone and called Sabrina, and she said "we're all ok, let me check on Gary Jr." Sabrina called right back! "Mom their alright!"

"what's happened," Janice told about the "door being stolen!"

Janice turned and told them "the kids are alright!"

Wade "Maria, Roland and two young boys were eating when I came through the kitchen, they told me how to get to your bedroom!" just then Gary Jr. and Brent walked into the bedroom with their side arms on with their badges clipped to the holsters, Gary Sr. Now I know were safe, the boy's are back in town!"

Wade looked at Gary Sr. "did you check on the other family?" Gary Sr. "said no," then he told "Gary Jr. and Brent to check with Roland to see if Hector and his family are all ok!"

Wade was looking at all the windows to see if he could tell how they had gotten into the house!

He look at all the door's and porches, and all the doors into the house, and he couldn't find any evidence of a forced entry!

Just then the phone rang, it was Brent, he said, "Hector is missing!"

His wife said "he roused her some time in the early morning and told her he though he heard something, but that she was so groggy, she went right back to sleep!"

Wade "oh shit," then said Whoops, "sorry Mrs. Pepper!"

But we better start looking for him, he could be wounded or even dead!

It's a good thing you folks didn't wake up while they were here stealing the door!"

"You could be dead! This smells like something our own Government might do!"

"To be specific the CIA, and their not suppose to be doing anything in the continental USA!"

Gary Sr. "let's split up and start looking for Hector!"

Gary Sr. sent Roland and his two boys checking the fencing around the Property, looking for Hector, and make sure the fence hadn't been berached!

Gary then sent Junior, Brent, Ben and Luke to check all around the house, looking for Hector, to check for any signs of any forced entry!

Wade and Gary took the golf cart down to the gate, Wade couldn't find any evidence of forced entry there eather!

But when Gary opened the gate, "he said "thank goodness, there sat Hector with duck tape around his leg, arms, and over his mouth!

Gary quickly got the tape off of Hector, and was checking him over, he had a rather large knot on his head, but Hector said "he was fine, but he didn't look to good, Wade "he needs to ge checked out by a Doctor!"

Gary "Janice is a retired nurse, and my Daughter is a nurse also. Lets take him up to the house and let them make that decision!"

When they got back up to the house, Hector's wife was so relieved to see him!

Wade ask "her to get Janice and Sabrina," when Rosie saw the knot on his head, she hugged him, and kissed him, told him, she "loved him," then she ran into the house!

And in a few seconds, they were back, Sabrina pulled a small light from her pocket, and ask Hector "to follow it with his eye's, she turned to her Mother "what do you think Mom?"

Janice "we should take him to a Doctor and make sure he's Ok!" she turned to Roland and ask "him to get the car." We need to take him to the emergency room, in Ashville!"

Janice, Sabrina, Rosie, Hector and Roland left for the Hospital. Wade "we really need to talk to Hector, to see, what he saw!"

Then Wade asked, do you have security cameras at the gate?"

Gary "I don't really know, we'll have to ask Roland, but I think we do."

Wade "lets go check the Gate!"

Gary opened them and Wade was looking, he turned and smiled, "you have a state of the arts, security camera here!"

"Where where do you keep the recording disks, for this camera?"

Gary "the only place I can think of would be the County Office, Uncle George made Stony Knob a county!"

Wade "yes I know that, I discovered that when I was checking on the Estate.

And ii ran it by some very smart Federal Lawyers and they thought it was a brilliant piece of legal work, should be put in the text books, and the Law **o**ffice he founded was impressed, with his work, had put it in the text books at Duke university, Law school!"

CHAPTER 12

As they got into the golf cart, Gary "I do know where the County office is because I'm the sheriff of this County, Gary laughed "go figure!"

Wade "so that's the reason your son and son-in-law were wearing firearms with badbes on them!"

Gary "yes, Roland and Hector are also Deputs, so whoever did this there will be charges brought against them, for beating a officer of the law."

Wade smiled, "I think when the President hears about this, there will be hell to pay, who ever is responsible for this!"

As they pulled up by the garage door, Gary raised the door and unlocked the office door!

Wade "I see them now," he showed them to Gary, Wade smiled at him, Gary

"Wade I've only been in this office once, and it's only been a week, since we got the place, I've just been enjoying my good fortune!"

"Right now I'm wishing I had never showed you the door, we only got to use it three times!"

"And that was to get the Grandkids and bring them up here with us, so we wouldn't have to drive back at night." As Gary was talking. Wade had the disk up and running, he paused it and said "I've got you, you S.O.B.," then he showed it to Gary. the camera showed two vehicles passing through the gate, and the VIN numbers on the suv's were visible, he enlarged them so they could be seen better!

Wade "with these, I'm sure we can find out who did this!"

He pulled out his cell phone, and called Sandy Lowe. Wade told "we've got a problem here, the door was stolen last night. I have some pictures from a surveillance camera, I'll fax them to you. I think we'll know who's behind this!"

Sandy asked "if anyone was hurt?" Wade "no sir, they were lucky, if it's who I think did this, they were damn lucky!"

Gary and Wade went back to the house, and Wade faxed the Pictures to Sandy Lowe, the head of the FBI!

When that was finished, Wade "I need a cup of coffee." they went to the kitchen, a pot of coffee was brewing, he had the cups out before Gary found the bacon and eggs in the warmer, Gary filled two plates, and they started eating!

Wade was telling Gary how sorry he was that this happened, I know you wished you hadn't told anyone about the door, but I feel you did the right thing and I feel sure we can get it back, and we can control it, Gary smiled

"Wade wait a minute, that door belong to me!

"If the Federal Government wants to buy it from me, then they can control the blasted thing!"

Wade "sorry but that thing is bigger than anything coming down the pike. if the Defense Department finds out about it's existence, they'll have to have it!"

Just then the girls came in from the Hospital. Gary ask "how's Hector?"

Janice "they did a cat-scan, his skull wasn't fractured, and he should be fine in a couple of hours!"

Wade "I want to talk to him, to see if he saw anything that would indicate who those people were." Wade and Gary walked over to Hector's house, when they got there, Rosie was putting him to bed, but she let them talk to him!

Wade ask "what did you see?" Hector "I woke up and thought I heard some body talking softly, when I got to the gate, I saw a group of men in black cloths, I thought it was strange, I told them, I have a gun, and told them they should move on and that when the light went out. But I did notice two large black SUV'S, and I woke up when the sun came up, and that's all I remember, until you took the tape off me Mr. Pepper, then he said I'm sorry!"

Gary "Wade Hound from the FBI, said we were all lucky to be alive, if they were who he thinks they were. They don't usually leave anyone alive to tell any tells!"

"Thank you Hector, but next time, try to alert all of us!"

And you take it easy, for a few days!"

Gary and Wade left Hectors house, Wade said "I think I'll go to the Ashville office, and see if Sandy's got anything from the photos I sent him. Would you mind if I came back this afternoon and spend a few more day with you? I don't think they'll be back, I think they got what they wanted, what I don't understand, is how the hell, did they find out about the door?

And I know you didn't tell anyone, Leonard, Sandy and the President and myself were the only people, who knew about the door!"

"If those photos don't give us anything, I'll have to start looking at them. But right now I trust all three of them with my life!" Wade shook his head

"Gary I'll see you this afternoon!"

Gary "come before supper and we can play some pool." Wade smiled "I would like that, see you later!"

And he was gone, Gary went to the County Office and got his gun. Roldand came in and said, "we need some ammo, he opened a draw that was full of for their weapons, we need several clips apiece, he got a Bank bag and put 9 clips in it, and gave it to Gary, he smiled just in case they come back, we'll be ready!"

Gary "Wade the FBI guy, will be coming back tonight. He thinks they've got what they wanted!"

Roland "what did they want in the house?" Gary "well Roland they got an antique That's very valuable, but Mr. Hound, thinks, with the security disk he found in the County Office, that they'll be able to recover the stolen item, then he ask Roland, if he knew, we had a recording system for the gate?"

Roland "yes sir! there are cameras all around the house, on the outside, I have to check them fairly often, to make sure that they're working and that we have plenty disks and keep it loaded and working! I would have told you about the system when I checked on them, I do that every 3 months!"

Gary smiled "I guess we need to set down and get me up to speed on the equipment around our home!"

And Roland you keep doing what you know needs to be done around here, and If you would like, we could look at your salary, to see if the County is paying you enough?"

Roland smiled "Sir I'm well compensated here, there are a lot of perks for us working for you and the former Mr. Pepper he was good to us when we needed it, and we feel you will be just as fair to us as he was!"

Gary "well Roland, I hope to be, and if you feel I'm not! you let me know.

Because I want you and yours to be as happy as we are!

All of this is new to me, and to be able to enjoy life. I owe that to my Great Uncle, that you knew better than I did. so we want you to be happy here and if you'll set up one day a week, for me and my son's, Gary Jr. and Brent to teach us what we need to know about Stony Knob!"

Roland replied "yes sir I will." Gary "because we think of you all as family, if you have problems, we have problems!"

Harry Ward The Dirctor Of The C.I.A.

He was telling one of his section Chiefs, "we have Merlin's door, but as yet we can't get it to do anything, so maybe, it was all hog wash, and the way we found it, was to simply followed Wade Hound. who the President put on the case! I knew if it could be found, Hound would find it!

So we put eyes at Stony Knob, and they saw the President at that location the Director of the FBI Sandy Lowe, and Walleye, and Hound, so I gave, the orders to snatch it, with as little damage as possible! one of the workers, came out to the gate, as we were entering it, Bobby had to knock him out, and taped him up. they were in and out in less then 25 minutes, the door is now in storage area in Langley, we've put our best brains on it, but as yet nothing!

And the President, better not find out who took it! everybody is breathing down my neck to cut cost, !Willie you keep me posted!"

Yes sir, and "oh yes I checked with, the White Staff and the President didn't leave his office last night, but a funny thing, is that Lowe and Walleye, left the White House, but there's no record of them checking in?"

"So how did they get there?"

Ward "we have photographs of them there, so the damn thing just might be working!"

"Keep them working with that damn thing, and remember, not a word to any one about this!"

"If this leaks out! I'll have your head, do you understand!"

Gary answered the phone, "Gary this is the President, Sandy Lowe just informed me that the door was taken last night!"

Gary "yes sir it was, Wade seems to think he knows who's got it. We found some photos, form the security cameras at the gate, he faxed them to Mr. Lowe, but I don't know how that turned out. Wade went to the Ashville office and hasn't returned yet. He told me he wanted, to stay for a few more days, just in case anything else happened! But I think he just likes it here, like we do!"

The President chuckled "I think your right, I find myself wanting to get back down there to, Gary I just wanted you to know, we had nothing to do with takeing that door, and we're working hard to find out who did this I'll have Sandy to keep you posted on our progress, you have a good day!"

Gary "thank you Mr. President, and you have a good day to!"

Gary hung up the phone! Sandy Lowe was in the video lab looking at the the VIN numbers Wade had faxed to him!

The Video techs had isolated VIN numbers and were running them through the systems, to get a fix on who in the Federal Government, they belonged finally they got a hit, they belonged to CIA, they were assigned to Langley and a agent named William Best, controlled them. it was Harry Wards right hand man!

Sandy "now that pisses me off, those a-holes, brought this up in the first place, if they wanted the door, why didn't they look for it instead of getting the President get us to look for it!

He turned his lab crew, "thanks guy's you're the best, give me all the paper work. I'm off to see the President, and Harry Ward will have hell to pay for this!"

He left the lab, called the President, when he answered, Sandy told him "we've found out who's behind the missing door!"

"Harry Ward, the SUV's were assigned to William Best. Ward's right hand man. There listed at Langley, how do you want to proceed with this sir?

I feel sure the door is somewhere at Langley!"

The President "well Harry can be a butt hole sometimes! But I'm not sure I want to can him just yet!"

Sandy "well sir if you'll give me permission, we at the FBI can get it back, give us a couple days!"

The President "Sandy you be careful. those guys can sometimes get trigger happy!"

Sandy "sir I'm well aware of how they operate, but my guys can out best at any thing they can throw at us!"

The President "well Sandy it all yours. Just keep me informed!"

Sandy replied "will do sir!" when the phone hit the cradle, he was on his Feet he said "we'll skunk the bastards! and they won't know we hit them."

He picked up they phone and dialed Wade, when Wade answered, Sandy told him "we know where the door is!"

"It was Wards outfit that snatche the door!" Wade "that bunch of bastard's"

Sandy "we've got to get it back," Wade "and do it in way, that they don't even know it's gone!"

Sandy "do you want to be in on it!" Wade "you damn right I do." Sandy "well get your butt, back to Washington!"

CHAPTER 13

Wade "I'll see you tomorrow!" Wade got into his car and drove back to Stony Knob. When he arrived it's was time for lunch, and as they were eating, Wade told the Peppers, "I have good news, we did find out who took Merlin's door!"

"And it was just as I thought it was, the CIA!" I'll spend the night here, and leave early in the morning, fly back to Washington, and get the door back!"

Gary "the President called and told me that he didn't have anything to do with the door being gone!"

He told me he was sorry that it happened, that he would get Mr. Lowe to keep me informed!"

Wade "the President is a good man, and you can count on him!"

Gary smiled "are you ready to get beaten in a game of pool, Mr. Hound?"

Wade laughed, "that remains to be sean, in my youth I was rather a good billiards player!"

Gary smiled "we'll just see about that," they played all afternoon, the games went back and forth, until they finslly called it a draw!

They finally ended up walking around on the property at Stony Knob, and talking about the door, Wade ask him, would you put a price on the door?"

Gary "how do you put a price on something like that?"

Wade ask "do you think, if one was quoted, you would be interested in selling it?

Gary "Wade I think if someone were to offer the right price they could buy it, right now, I have no idea what that could be!"

Ben came out and told them "supper is ready, and Nana said you guys were to come in and eat!"

They drifted into the dinning room, sat down, began eating and chatting.

As the evening wore on, Wade said "I'm going to call it a night, I have an early flight back to Washington in the morning!"

When Gary got up the next morning, Wade was already gone, as he was eating breakfast, he told "Janice that Wade had ask him about selling the door, what do you think about that?" she thought about it, then said "well honey, I don't want to keep something around, we have to worry about all the time, I wished we had never told anyone about the darn thing!"

Gary "honey we didn't tell anyone, the man came looking for it, but your right we probably, shouldn't have to Wade!"

When Wade got off the plane, in Washington D. C., there was a car waiting to take him to the F.B.I. headquarters at the Hover Building. When he arrived there Sandy Lowe, was waiting for him with 10 other agents, they were ready to start mapping out a plan to get the door back. Wade went around shaking hands, with all of them!

He had worked with all of them on different cases in the past. Sandy said "you guys know, we have to come up with a plan, that we can execute so well, that those knuckle heads, over at Langley, will never know we did it!"

Sandy "Wade I want you to take charge of this operation, so lets start brain-storming this into being!"

Wade "do we know how they're cleaning the building? and can we sneak into the building as a cleaning crew?"

#2 "do they have a contract crew that cleans the place?"

Sandy spoke up and said "I have a new architecture rendering of the build-ing, and he passed them around so each one could have a copy!

Then said "you people didn't see these in the FBI building. Did everyone hear that?"

And all around the room he heard yes sir's. Troy, one of the guy's "it look like they have the building well locked down!"

"But if we knew where they're storing it?" a phone rang and Sandy answered it, and was mumbling into it, then he said, "very good, and thanks I owe you one!"

Sandy came back to the table and said Wade, "the darn thing is this storage area, pointing it out on the architects drawing, close to this wall." Wade "dose that answer your question Troy?"

Then they all started looking for the shortest route to that location, from they could enter the building!

Robin, another one of the guys, shut his cell phone and said "they do have a contract cleaning crew, that comes in at 10 o'clock p.m., the name of the company is Clean Well Services!"

Wade "that's how we get into their house!" Wade "this is where the cleaning crew enters the building, and the proximity of the storage area, from where they enter the building, is very close!"

Wade smiled "we should be in and out in less than 10 minutes!"

Wade "we'll need profiles on those people, we need to look just like them in order to get through the gate, and the Military Guards. And we need to find out who's posted for the next couple of days. Do we need to neutralize them?"

Wade "Robin, you and Lester find out about the military. Mark, Troy and Alvin, check on the van's and he personal! Mick, you come up with some-thing from our chemical line, that will put them to sleep for at least 30 min. and when they do wake up, they want remember, so they don't know, they were out for that length of time, can we all handle this!"

They all replied "yes sir!"

"Now remember, the CIA is one of the worlds best at Skullduggery. But we will show them how it's done, and that the FBI is second to none!"

The plan worked perfectly, they executed it a day and a halh later. And at present, the door was under heavy security at the FBI hHq. building." The C.I.A. was still scratching their heads, how this could have happened on there watch!

Ward started started, cracking heads as soon as he found out the door was Missing!

The FBI had their best minds working at getting the door to work for them.

When they couldn't get it to work for them. Sandy reported this to the President!

That they had the door, but couldn't get it to work for them. The President told "Sandy, to get Gary and Janice Pepper to come to Washington, D.C. for a visit!" And they can stay at the White House for a few days. My Wife will like Janice Pepper, she's not a pretentious lady and Gary is just a fine person to be around. As you know this town is full of stuffed shirts and B-holes, get Wade, to get them up here!"

Sandy had given Wade the responsible of telling the Peppers, that the door had been found and was in the FBI building and secured!

Wade flew home to Ashville, when he got to his house, there were two cars parked in front of the house!

He knew who they were. He started not to go into the house, but had second thoughts, that maybe they would be through and would leave shortly. It was a school night and he knew Jack would watching his son closely, that he would have him on a curfew, it was almost 9 thirty!

He checked the Pool area they were not there, so he went into the house quietly.

He two young people, moaning after making love, in one of the bedrooms, and he would not interrupt them! it brought back fond memories of his love, when they were in school and living together!

He quietly walked back out the door and quietly left and headed for Stony Knob. As he was driving along, he called the Peppers, one of the grandkids answered the phone, he ask to speak to Gary Sr., when he picked up the phone. Wade "I'm headed you way, could I spend the night at you place?"

Gary chuckled "Wade you're like home folks around here, of coarse you can!"

As he pulled up in front of the main house, and got out, when he got to the front door, Gary opened it and asked him "if he was hungry, and told him that the rest of the family were in the kitchen, foraging for food. when he got there, every one was munching on something. They all said hi, but kept on eating!

Gary "its every man for himself." Janice, Wade if its not on the table look in the Fridge, and if its not there, you'll have to call the pizza guy!"

Wade "Gary's already told me that its every man for himself, I know the rules." When they were through eating and cleaning up after themselves.

Most of them had gone to the game room to play!

Wade "I have to talk to you two, we have the door back, its in the Hoover building in a safe place! We learned that the CIA had tried to use it, but couldn't get it to work for them, when we got it back, the FBI put their best technicians on it, and they couldn't get it to work either. And the President would like for you both to come to Washington for a visit, you'll be staying in the White House, as his guest for a few days!"

They look at each other and smiled, then Janice "I think it would be a fun thing to do!"

Gary smiled "when do we leave." Wade smiled "is tomorrow to soon? The President's calender is clear for the next three day's, he thought you would like staying with him and his wife!

And he could talk to you about the door!"

"Wade I don't know much about the old door. Other than what Mrs. Pepper wrote about it. I guess we could take what she's written, about the door. She wanted to publish a book, to prove that the door was real!

But they realized it would be very dangerous to publish any thing on the Door even if it did prove, Arthur and Merlin did live, in the past. And they decided to just keep it quiet!

And to use the door for their own entertainment!" And from the experience we've had. I can't say that I blame them!"

Wade "I think I'm going to bed." Janice ask "what time are we expected to be at the Whie House?"

Wade answered, "well anytime we get there. We could leave at 8 thirty, the flight time is only 30 to 45 minutes, we could be in White House by 10 to 10:30 dose the sound like a good plan?"

Janice "that sounds ok for us." Gary "Wade, the President dose know we're just plain people, doesn't he?"

"Sure, we've inherited a few dollars but that hasn't really sunk in just yet!"

Wade laughed "Gary, I think that's why he liked you when he first met you coming through the door. You're not pretentious, your just good folks."

Wade "I've heard him say once that Washington was full stuff shirts and B-holes. He and his wife just happened to end up in the White House. I think you know he's a good man!"

Gary and Janice were packed and ready to go by 7 thirty, Janice had put one of the dresses, that had belonged to the former Mrs. Pepper in the suitcase, just in case!

She need something formal to wear, she made Papa pack a suit in suitcase, just incase he need one. They were in the air by 9 o'clock. Wade and Janice were talking, Gary had his eyes closed and was deep in thought. He was thinking about all the things that had happened to him in only a couple of weeks, and that he was on a Government plane, going to see the President of the United States of America!

And just a short time ago he lived in a house by a railroad track, thinking he was doing ok. But now he knew that his children were secure in their futures!

And that made him smile. Janice shook his arm and ask "what are you smiling about old man!"

He opened his eyes and whispered into her ear, "guess who's going to get laid in the White House tonight?"

Janice smiled "who?" He smiled at her and said, "me! That's who! Janice poked him on his arm, "maybe if you're good!" She put her finger to her lips, in other words be quiet!

CHAPTER 14

Wade had already got the drift of their conversation, and was smiling at them. when they landed and taxied to a stop, a car was waiting for them.

When their luggage was loaded in the trunk of the car, and they got into it!

Wade told the driver "to take them to the Hoover building, that Sandy Lowe wanted to talk to Gary and Janice about the door!

The traffice was heavy, this time of the day. It took them a good 30 minutes to get to the Hoover Building!

Wade had a cart pick them up in the parking garage, and as they drove through the maze of the under ground parking lot!

When they finally got to the employee entrance, Gary told Wade "don't ask me to find my way back to where we just came from!"

Wade smiled "I know what you mean, when I first went to work here, it took almost 2 months to learn how to get in and out this place. But after a while it became second nature to me. Now I think I could get in and out of here blindfolded!"

The Secretary, at the deak, outside the Director's office. "Told Wade to go right in, the Director was waiting for them!"

Wade "you already know, Sandy, and this Dr. Flitter, and Dr. Ricker, these two educated fellow's wanted to meet the owners of Merlin's door, they've been trying to get the door to work for them. But haven't had any success.

They want to know how you two, get it to work!"

Gary smiled "we don't know eather. Gary replied "According to the reading material we have, say's that the possesses this door can go anywhere they desire. We've only it four times. The first time, was to get the Grandchildren up to our New Home at Stony Knob, we went to our home in Stanley first, our kids were to get their cars, and go pick up their kids, and drive back up to Stony Knob, then I thought, rather than my son and daughter having to drive all that distance, why not collect the Grandchildren, that way,

I decided we just take them through the door, and that's what we did! by the way Mr. Lowe, the more people that know about this darn door, the more trouble there's going to be. Now we know the CIA knows, and there could several other people and add that to the FBI people that know about it. You people are beginning to scare the hell out of me. Do you realize what that darn thing is capable of!"

Wade ask "Gary to settle down, they were just trying to make it work!"

Then Gary "yes but how many more people know?" Sandy "the CIA thinks it's a dud, and our own people think so to!"

Gary Mr. Lowe do you think it's a dud?" "Wade do you?" They both shook there heads no, Gary "well I think we should talk to the President and see what he thinks. Now show me the door. And I'll take us there now!"

Janice "Wade get us something cold to drink, I think the old man is flustered!" and she laughed!

The tension in the room began to wan. Sandy looked at Gary "what would you like to drink, Beer, Wine or scotch!"

Wade laughed "Sir we don't want to give this man any booze, he might just start tap-dancing for us." and the whole room, started laughing! Gary looked at Wade "Now that was a good one Wade!"

Sandy "name your poison!" Janice "a diet sundrop for us. and if you can't get that, any caffeine free drink will do!" in a matter of minutes, they were drinking something cold, and setting around the table talking about food! until Gary "are we going to see my door?" Wade looked at his watch, "we should go see the President. He he ask that we be there at 12 o'clock!"

"and the traffic is horrendous out there today." Gary looked at them and said the door!"

Do you mind if Dr. Flitter and Dr. Ricker go with us?"

Gary looked puzzled at them, Mr. Lowe, do you have complete confidence in these two men?"

Sandy "yes sir I do." Gary looked at the two Doctors, the reason I'm asking, "if they know my wife and I can use the door, will it go any further?

Because I think that puts Janice and I in a sticky position," Sandy "I see what mean. I think from now on you two will have to have protection!"

Gary "oh crap, and looked at Janice and said, tell me what to do Babe?"

Janice smiled "maybe your just a worry wart, could we get on with please!"

They all went somewhere, that Gary knew he wouldn't be able to retrace his way back, to where they came from!

Gary pulled his wife close and whispered, what have we got ourselves into Maw, Janice looked at him, smiled "we're secret agents, known as Ma and Paw Pepper!"

And that tickled Gary all the way down to his socks, and they both started laughing and couldn't stop!

Then the whole party stopped, and were looking at them strangly, then Wade started next, he had contagious laughter, and before long, they were all were holding their sides and leaning against the wall, for a good 3 minutes!

Until Sandy got controll of himself, "OK, OK, Stop it!"

When they finally stopped, they were wiping their eyes. Wade pointed his finger at Gary and Janice!

"Chief, its all there fault." Sandy "I don't think that kind of laughter has ever happened in this building, but it was refreshing!" He looked at Gary and Janice. "I'm not going to ask what that was all about, because if we get started again, we'll be late for the big Chief!"

"And he might just fire us all." And the next door they came to, Sandy used a card, finger print and voice recognition, to get it open, there were 2 military guards setting behind a desk!

They had to see, FBI ID's and sign a log book. after that Sandy showed Gary and Janice and there had only been 3 people's logged in. thay were the two Doctors and Sandy's name were written on the log book!

Sandy "we've been very tight with, security and access to this unit! and he pulled out his card again and opened the next door, when the entered the room Gary saw the old door and walked over to look for any damage to Gary said "it looks okey to me Babe!"

One of the Doctors said "we did take a core sample to verify the age of the door, with carbon dating! and we found that it came from the area that Legend says Merlin and King Arthur lived!

Gary "supposedly, I think as smart as you people are, you would surmise that this evidence is proof that Merlin and Arthur did live a very long time, ago!"

"Yes, we could, but we couldn't find any kind of enegery that would indicate, the door could do anything like we were told it would!"

Gary "all we know is what my graet Aunt had written about it. and they realized how dangerous it could be for her to publish anything about the the door!"

"that their safety, by owning the door would be at risk. because of what the door could do. They decided to use it at their own conveniece and amusement! they actually used it quiet frequently. which is what I would like to do! she said in her writings that they went all over the world. they'd go out in the evening. Some times to Monte Carlo, they like to play the slots and that was her favorite place. and I like to play them to, and was looking forward to going there also. before all of this happened!"

Wade "Gary we should think about going to the White House!" Gary "lets go, I suppose the Oval Office!"

Sandy "that's right, the President is waiting for us there now!"

Gary "honey would you do the honors, she walked over, opened the door to the Oval Office of the White House!"

She turned and ask if the two Doctors would like to see the President setting at his desk. they were looking bug eyed, not beliving what they were seeing!"

Janice "Mr. Lowe, Mr. Hound, would you be our guest, the Doctors have to stay unless they've been invited!"

Sandy looked at them "sorry fellows, you have to leave that way, pointed at the door they came in!"

Janice, Gary, Sandy and Wade, stepped into the Oval Office, the President stood up, saying WOW "I thought you guys would be coming through the other door, when you arrived." Sandy "sorry sir, Wade told me that the Pepper's were to be here at 12 p. m., he looked at his watch, just in the nick of time!"

Gary smiled at them and said, "let me try something!"

He went back to the door put his hands on the frame of the door, gave it a strong healthy tug. When the door came at him quickly, he had to stop it to keep it from rolling into the furniture in the Oval Office, he said "woe-ha" as he stopped it!

Gary smiled this thing belongs to the Peppers, and it seems it only works for I think it should be with us. Dose anyone have any objections about it being here ?"

Wade shook his head NO, Sandy looked at the President, Andrew "don't look at me, it belongs to Gary and Janice Pepper, and they're my guest. He walked over to the wall the door came out of to see if there was any damage to the wall and there was none. Then he was inspecting the door, from every angle, then he finally "this thing is truly magic!"

Janice Mr. Lowe, you should alert, your people, that the door is no longer in the Hoover Building, before they start to panic, about it being gone!"

Sandy "you're right, I told them heads would rool if it disappeard! And it did just disappeard!" Sandy flipped his cell phone, and started talking to someone at the Hoover building!

Wade "I think Gary should eat something, he looking a little peaked!"

"and I'm about to starve myself!"

The President, "what would you like to eat? We'll go up to my quarters, I'll call Kathy and let her know you're here. Wade you and Sandy are welcome to, he walked over to his desk, picked up the phone and called his wife

"Honey, the Pepper's are here, we're on our way up for lunch. Wade and Sandy will be eating with us to!"

He layed the phone in the cradle, smiling Wade she said she'd throw another chicken leg on the fire just for you guy's!"

Andrew looked at Gary and Janice and said, "I think the door's safe here in this Oval office!"

He ushered them out of the Oval office. The Staff and the Secret Service people were looking unsure. Four were coming out of the office with the President. They had not seen anyone go in, and no one had signed in. When the President saw the looks on their faces. "He said relax, you all know Mr.

Lowe and Wade Hound. and these two are my guest, Mr. and Mrs. Pepper he turned and told the head of his Secret Service detail, "let no one go into my office, unless I say so!"

The President lead them into the private portion of the White House. He introduced his wife to them, and the Pepper's to her!

Cathy "do you mind if I hug you? Andrew has talked so much about you, I feel like I know you already. Andrew say's you are fine people. She hug them both." Then she looked at Wade and Sandy, smiled "no, but maybe another time. she said to Janice "I think of them as faimly." Gary "Wade is special to us even though, he started all this ruckus with our Antique door!"

Cathy "Andrew told me about it, and it sounds like a fantasy. I would like to see it!"

The President laughed "its in my office." Cathy smiled "after we eat I'll have to see it!"

CHAPTER 15

Then Cathy lead them into the dinning room, they sat down, Gary and Wade hardly spoke, they were stuffing their faces. When everyone was full and satisfied. the First Lady was inquiring about Pepper family, Janice was telling her all about her two children and the three Garndchildren, who were living with them now at Stony Knob. That each one has their own apartment

The house is rather large, you must come for a visit. Cathy "I'd like that, sometimes it's good to get away from Washington!"

Gary ask "if she would like to see the door, before nap time, because I'm full and contented. I know it early, but as I mature, I find that maps seem to sneak up on me!"

Sandy chuckled "I know what you mean, I'm feeling the same!" They all looked at Wade and his eyes were closed!" all of the laughed! Wade opened his eyes and said. "I was only resting my eyes, thank you!"

The President "yes Wade we know how that is!"

"Then he ask Cathy if she would like to see Merlin door. She repied "yes I would if I could, Please!"

They all got up, to go, Sandy "Wade and I should go!" Wade "wait a minute, I don't live in Washington anymore, he looked at Sandy "I guess you'll have to put me up for a few days!"

The President "you'll stay in the White House with us! and Sandy I need to talk to you about another matter, we can discuss it later this afternoon!"

Sandy "I'll have to go with you to the Oval Office, I don't have a ride back to the Hoover building, where my car is parked!" Andrew lead the way back to the Oval Office!

Janice was now calling the first Lady, Cathy, she was charming, warm and a friendly person!

Cathy and Janice became friends immediately!

While they were all walking down to the Oval Office. Wade, Sandy and Gary were talking to the President, at one point. Gary called Mr. President,

Andrew stopped them, then said, "I'm the President, but my name is Andrew Mellon, Gary please call me by mine name, especially when we together, as friends, which I think are!" he shook Gary hand "you're my kind of people, and were already Friends look at our wives their all ready buzzing like bee's together!

Gary "yes sir I feel were we are already friends, but if I should slip and call you Mr. President please forgive me!"

As they reached the Oval Office, the President stopped and talked to his staff and the Secret Service, telling "them he was not to be disturb for the next 4 hours and possibly more!"

Gary surmised that he wanted to use the door, after we got Sandy back to the Hoover Building. Cathy was still in awe, after she saw Sandy leave through the door and into the Hoover Building!

Janice ask her "where she would like to go," she looked at Andrew. he smiled "its your choice Mrs. Mellon!"

Wade "sir we shouldn't leave our Country." Janice spoke up and said "would you like to see our place in North Carolina. it's a compound, you would be safe there!"

Gary "and I could take the door back home where it belongs!"

Cathy walked around the door, and said "its hard to belive, how it can do what it dose!"

Andrew "the proof is in the pudding, Love!" Cathty "Andrew told me you like to play the slot machines." Gary smiled "yes we do, but I think you two would stick out like a sore thumb in a casino. but if you could change your appearance and would like to try it!"

"We could give it a try!" Andrew smiled "I think we should stay away from the gambling Mrs. Mellon!

Cathy laughed "I think it would be a fun thing to do!

Then Cathy ask is there anyone at Camp David?" Andrew "we keep a staff there, but we always let them know when we're coming! That might not be a good idea to just drop in!

Cathy "well if your worried about security." she looked over a Wade "we have quick draw McGraw with us!"

Wade laughed at hearing that, then he said, "Andrew, I can handle security Sir!"

Andrew "honey, I don't want to go there please, lets just go to the Pepper Home in North Carolina for your first experience with the door!"

Cathy "oh alright," Janice smiled "I know you'll love it, she walked over to the door. Lets all go to North Carolina!"

She opened the door, and took Cathy's hand, "I want you to meet my family!"

They can't see us yet. it appeared, the whole family was eating something and watching television in the den!

Janice and Cathy into the den, with Wade, and the President and Gary bring-ing up the rear. and for a minute, Gary Jr., Sherry, Sabrina and Brent didn't see them enter the room!

Then Sabrina jumped up and said, "well look who just arrived." Gary Sr.

Ask "what are you guy's watching on the tube, and what are you eating, we want some to!

Gary Jr. replied, "strawberry ice cream. Maria made it for us." Janice "I want you to me the First Lady, then she introduced Cathy to them all." And they welcomed her to Stony Knob, Cathy "I'd love to have some of that strawberry ice cream, after that trip from Washington to North Carolina, she smiled I need some refreshments!"

Sherry got up "let me get you some, Mr. President, would you and Wade like some to!"

"I know Mon and Dad will eat some!" the kids were watching a Carolina Panther football game, they all eat their ice cream, Gary ask "Andrew would you and Cathy like to go out side, it looks like a beautiful day out! or would you like to go out on our deck, it has a beautiful view from it!"

It's just out side our bedroom!"

Janice "I want you to see how beautiful it is here at Stony Knob, and they left the noise bunch watching the foot ball game, Gary lead them out through their bedroom, Cathy though their bedroom was lovely, but when she saw how beautiful the scenery was from the Pepper's porch, they sat and enjoyed the quiet and peacefulness, setting and chatting like norman every day people!

Andrew "Gary you have a very beautiful place here at Stony Knob." Cathy smiled as cool breeze ruffled the flowers setting around the deck, then said "I just love it here!"

Janice smiled "you can come any time you wish, just let me know. you know just how easy it was to get here, I would love for you to come!

Carhy "Andrew, when things get a little dicey in Washington it would nice to get away from it here, no one would have to know!"

Andrew smiled "I would like that very much!"

Gary "Sir, you know we would love for you to think of this place as a home away from home!"

For a few minutes, there was silence, as they were taking in the sights and sounds of Stony Knob!

But it was not to last, Gary had fallen to sleep and started to snoring, it was a moderate snore, but as soon as the rest of them realized, who it was, Janice

"Papa wake up your snoring in front of our guest!"

Gary smiled "I'm sorry Mr. President! It's Cathy fault, she fed me so well, at lunch, and I guess the ice cream, just put me to sleep! but it was rude of me and I'm very sorry, maybe I need to move around a bit, Andrew would you like to take walk. and Ladies, you might like to take a stroll with us that is if we have time?"

Andrew chuckled "Gary I was almost ready to nod off myself. as for the time, we've got at least 2 more hours, before we need to get back to the White house!"

Andrew and Cathy, Gary and Janice, walked hand in hand up to the best view of Stony Knob!

At the top of the mountain they found a nice setting rock and sat and to enjoyed the view!

Cathy "its so peaceful here, it would make a person, want to take a nap! or read a good book, or think of other things." she looked at Andrew and smiled, Andrew got the drift, and he smiled!

Then he look at his watch, do you realize how long we've been setting here? its been almost two hour. If I don't respond soon the chaps out side my door, will get real excited. and as nice as this is, we had better get back to the White House!

They strolled back down to the house, walked into the den, told the kids by collected Wade who was napping, Andrew walked over to him and tapped him on his shoulder, and he almost jumped up, but when he saw who it was he smiled, "just resting my eyes sir!"

Gary chuckled "Wade that wasn't just resting your eyes, that was snoring and I mean big time stuff!"

Janice "Wade don't pay him any attention, we had to wake him up earlier he said it was Cathy fault, and the ice cream!"

Andrew "we're ready to go back to the White House!" Wade "sir if its alright with you, I'd like to stay here for the night and go home to Ashville in the morning!"

The President "I'm sorry Wade, but we need to talk, just wait until we can discuss some issues!"

Wade understood what he was talking about and said "yes Sir, I understand, I'm ready to go sir!"

Gary "Andrew would you mind if I bring the back home sir?" Andrew "just as long as we can get back home ourselves!" Gary went over to the wall they came from, put both hands on the door frame, and gave it a good strong And the door was now back in Stony Knob, where it belongs. Cathy ask "can we get back to the White House?" Janice "yes honey, we can Merlins door will just be at Stony Knob, where it belongs!"

Cathy "but can we all go back, to the White House!" Gary "now that the door is here, where in the White House, would you like to go?"

Andrew "we should go back to the Oval Office. The Secret Service personal will go bananas, if we don't return to the last place they knew we were!"

Gary "let me get my son, to put the door back into the safe, he called Gary Jr. and ask him "to put the door back into the safe, when Gary put the door back into the safe!"

They had all followed Gary Jr. into the closet, where the safe was! After that was accomplished! Gary opened the door into the Oval Office!

Cathy smiled "I could get use to traveling like this!"

Wade "sir it's been 4 hours, we should make an appearance for the troops."

They left the Oval Office, the Presedent ask his personnel "if any messages been left for him!" there were none!

Carhy stopped them and said "what do you guys think of sleeping in Abe's bedroom." Janice "the Lincoln bedroom" she smiled "I would love to sleep There." Janice looked at Gary and smiled and winked. Gary smiled, I think that means, I'm going to get lucky in the old boy's bed!

Cathy showed them the way to the Lincoln bedroom, and showed them where anything they needed was, she told "them Dinner would be served in your room!"

When the door closed, Gary went swiftly across the room and dove onto the Lincoln bed!

Janice "you shouldn't do that, its an old bed, you might break it!"

Gary laughed "if its in the White House, I'm sure its in good shape for the shape its in," and laughed!

Janice was looking around the room at the paintings and the furniture, She said "isn't awesome!"

Gary "do you really think so. remember your from the South! and that old boy stopped on us really good!"

Janice sat down on one of the chairs in the room and was looking and think-ing of where she was. Gary got up off the bed, "I need a shower, and left her setting, just looking around the room!

CHAPTER 16

He found all he needed to take a shower, got his pajamas for after the shower, he was enjoying the warmth of the water, when a lovely lady joined in the shower, and to him that made life all right in his book! they ate a late dinner. and went to bed, and they did have a good time in old Abe's bed!

The next morning, Gary was up in the bathroom, when someone knocked on their door, he found his robe, put it on, went to the door, opened it and there stood a Maid with a cart, she said good morning "I have your breakfast and a note from the First Lady, with an itinerary on it!" she pushed the cart into the room, said "have a good day!" Gary poured a her a cup of coffee, and put it under nose. She opened her eyes, smiled said "good morning love, I belive we had a good night! Gary "that we did Babe!" Janice sat up, she was naked, Gary smiled and tossed her bath robe, you'd better cover that up before I get excited, and want to come back to bed with you!"

Janice smiled "oh no you want old man! he gave her the note from Cathy

Janice said "they would not be traveling with them today. That Wade would take them on a tour of Washington and show them all the Historical places in the Capitol city, and they could start whenever they were ready!

And they were ready at 9:30, just as they finished dressing, there was a knock on their door. Janice opened it was Wade, he smiled "good morning, you look happy and fresh this morning!"

Janice smiled "I feel good thank you! And you look spiffy to Wade!" Gary asked "why the President wasn't coming with them today?"

Wade replied "Andrew thought you might see more of Washington with out all the hoop la of a Presidental Motercade all through the city!

I'm to take you anywhere you want to go. Gary "I've always wanted to go to the Smithsonian, but with 14 museums, it would take more than 3 day to see it all!"

They left the White House, Wade took them to the Capital building and the Library of Congress!

That took a good half of the day. They went back to the White House and had Lunch with the President and First Lady! from there they went to Smithsonian, Gary though what a wonderful place browse through!

But it wasn't long until, Wade said "Janice is wanting to leave, that she was getting tired!"

They had been in it all afternoon. As they were driving back to the White House!

Gary "Wade, if we had been shopping she wouldn't complain of being tired!"

Wade "you're probably right, maybe we should do that tomorrow.

Washington has some very nice Mall's to shop in!"

At Supper with Andrew and Cathy in their quarters, after they had finished eating. the President took them into their lounge. Sat them down and told that he was assigning them protection. And Wade had already agreed to be one of them. He would be responsible for choosing two other's from with-in FBI The Field office in Ashville would be the back up team for him!"

Gary "do you think that's needed?" Andrew "yes we do, the problems, with the CIA. There also NSA and all the other Agencies that would love to be able to utilize your door. by just walking through it!

What we would like is to make it accessible to all the Agencies to use!

I myself would like to make use of it. It would be more secure than anything available to the Presidency as yet. and more cost effective, and would make you a very rich man! If we were to put those funds into an account somewhere that only you could access! Andrew "Gary you and Janice just think about it overnight and we will talk about it in the morning. You don't have to respond tonight! And we'll talk more in the morning is that ok with you!"

Gary and Wade left together. Janice was still talking Cathy, just out side the lounge!

Gary ask "Wade do you think about all this crap?" Wade responded "well you are in a position to be of great service to your Country!"

The President was right to you under his protection, I don't think you fully realize the impact that thing will have on the every day working of the Federal Government! As far as we know, you and Janice are the only people who can operate Merlin's door! So they will have to build something at Stony Knob, with your permission and approval of coarse!" Wade added

"just wait until morning, before you make up your mind about any of this OK!"

Janice walked up behind them and ask "what are you guy's talking about. Papa you looked awfully serious!"

Wade "we were just talking about looking for a good Mall tomorrow, what do you think about that?" Janice smiled, "I think that's a good idea, I haven't got the kids anything from Washington!"

Wade "you mean Cathy hasn't given anything that belongs to the President? He's got all kinds of goodies!"

Janice "I'll ask Carhy tomorrow." Wade escorted them to the Lincoln room and told them goodnight!

As they shut the door! Gary "honey what do you think about all this? I'm not sure where this is going. Did you not understand what Andrew was say-ing at the table? Were the only one's that can operate the door. Therefore you or I will have to activate it for anything they want to do with it. And I don't want to be put on the spot 24/7 for the Federal Government! what do you think?"

Janice responded with, "maybe we should try to find out, if anyone else in the family, can get it to work? Sabrina and Gary Jr. are next in line in our Wills. Maybe they could get it to work for them! But we should talk to them about it first!

Janice "I'm taking a shower first, Buster!" and as he watched her remove her cloths, Merlin's door drifted from his mind, he smiled, another good night in Abe's bed, the next morning he woke up with a smile on his face.

Janice looked at him smiling "your just a horny old man!" He smiled again "Yea, I guess you could say that!"

After they both has showered and dressed for the day. There was a knock on the door. Gary went to the door thinking, that it was breakfast. But it was Wade!

He said the President wanted to have breakfast with you this morning. He has some plans for Merlin's Door, he would like to talk to you about." Gary "we are going shopping? this is for Janice, you know she was looking forward to it!"

They went to the President Quarters, and had breakfast, with Andrew and Cathy. after they finished eating!

Janice and Cathy were talking about girly stuff. Andrew said "Gary, I want to build something at Stony Knob to protect Merlin's Door, and I hope you will give me permission to build something there! "lets all go down to the Oval Office," "I want to talk more about Merlins Door!"

Cathy and Janice, Wade, Gary and Andrew, as they were walking, down to the Oval Office two young men joined them. The President introduced Them to Gary and Janice, this is Marc Sprinkle, and Larry Short, Wade picked them out of quiet a few young men at the FBI! Wade think's they are total packages! with brains and are strong young men!"

They both shook hands with Gary and Janice, they both responded with "please to meet you Mr. and Mrs. Pepper!"

Gary smiled "Marc you look a lot like my son Gary Jr. we would like to welcome you aboard what ever train this is!"

They walked into the Oval Office. there were four other people in the room, and as soon as we entered, they all stood up and Andrew "introduced them Architect's, first, Saul Frankle and Woodrow Call. the other two are contractors, Jessy Hartwell, and Ralph Childers!"

Andrew "Saul let see what you've come up. would you start first and show us what you have!"

Mr. Frankle, put up his plans, "we took a satellite survey of Stony Knob to get the best placement of the compound, he pointed to the parcel of land he wanted to build on. "The President has asked for comfortable quarters for his wife and himself. And comfortable quarters for a platoon of Marines!

The building, will be self contaned, electricity, water, oh as I understand, that Mr. Pepper already has a water recycling system in place!

We will have the same system for this unit, and air system second to none!

From the air it will look like a barn. There will be two levels below the barn Structure, and it will be made of a new Polymer, stronger that steel, it will be a foot thick, the Barn portion will look like rock, just like the house. the lowest level will be for parking, but the rest will be comfortable living quarters!

Now to do the job, we will have to make a road, on the out side of existing fence to where we enter the Property. We'll install a gate and when the project is finished. take it out and remove the road and install a driveway from the main gate at the house to the barn, that Mr. President is our prop-osal!"

Mr. Call had a round shape cone type building, that would be underground with nothing visible above ground. He gave a good pitch for his project.

But Gary would have nothing to do with it. And when the Preaident ask him to chose, he chose the barn concept!

Gary ask Mr. Frankle, how long would take to finish this project?" he rep-lied, "three months tops, but if we have both contractor's working for us, we could shorten the time!"

Andrew said "I would like this project to be finished as soon as possible."

Mr. Frankle smiled and said, "you got it Mr. President!"

Andrew said "and no one is to know this is Govrenment project. No publ-icity. Or fanfare, what so ever!"

In 2 and a half months, the project was completed, with Gary and the President's full approval!

The Federal Government started using the door a week after the bunker was finished. Wade, Marc and Larry, had a pistol range build above the bunker.

Gary Sr. and Gary Jr., Brent, Roland and Hector, they all became Marksmen with their wepons, their shooting was as good as the 3 FBI Agents. The President declared Stony Knob a Federal procted land!

And a platoon of Marines were assigned to guard the compond!

One of the missions through the door, nabbed one of the Worlds most wanted men O.B. L.! When Gary first saw him, he thought what a sorry piece of crap!

But as soon as arrived, he was whisked away from Stony Knob to who knew where. Gary ask "Wade, where have taken him?"

Wade responded with "I don't know myself," then he said "but most likely to Cuba with the rest of the Arab's!"

But there were fun times for Gary and Janice. Wade, Mark and Larry escr-orted them to Las Vegas for 8 hours to play the slots. And they all returned home with Money in their pockets!

Gary knew they knew they would go again!

The President visited often. Cathy and Janice became good friends, Cathy loved the piece and tranquility of Stony Knob!

Gary Sr. thought that Merlin's door was going to be a pain in the butt, but it hadn't been!

The Federal Government was using it more often, and he was being very well compensated!

The C.I.A./ F.B.I /N.S.A./ H.L.S had given the Pepper family awards for their service to their country!

CHAPTER 17

Gary Sr., Gary Jr., and Brent built a shop to tinker in under the house, had invented a heat seeking bullet. The 3 of them had developed it. they talked to the President and gave him a thorough demonstration of the bullet.

He was so impressed with the concept, "he told them, he would tell the Defense Dept. and he was sure they would want it in their arsenel of wepons!"

Andrew suggested "that they put a patent on the bullet." And as soon as that was completed!

The President showed it to the Defense Dept. And they wanted all they could manufacture. Together the Pepper Family purchased an old Mill that was structurally sound, and started manufacturing the products, for what it would cost them for meterals, they needed to manufacture the product, plus materials for making the product, plus labor cost, and maintenance of the facility, plus their profit $??. per every 1000 rounds sold to the Government The Defense Dept. was so impressed with the offer!

They provided the Security, plus hired all the management and work force. For the Pepper Arm's Manufacturing Co. the Federal Government put the plant under Federal Juridiction!

So the Town of Weaverville or the State of North Carlonia could not tax the revenue of the Plant!

Gary Sr., Brent, and Gary Jr. were on the Board of Governors of the Plant but didn't run the Company!

They just collected their portion of the Profits from the selling of the munitions. Which was quiet substantial!

They were selling well into the billions of rounds and would be in the trillions!

Every Law Enforcement agency in the United States wanted to buy them. plus our Allies around the world were purchasing them!

And on rare occasions if the munitions were needed badly they were delivered through Merlin's Door. That was called sameday delivery, and there was an extra charge for that kind of service!

Wade didn't like the door being used for that kind of business, and he let every one in the chain of command know what he thought about it. Sandy told him "not to worry that it wouldn't be used on a regular bases, just on rare occasions, when the need was there!"

But Gary approved the use for that purpose. Wade talked to Gary Sr. "about not letting the munitions go through the door, that it brought to much attention to something that we want to keep a secret!"

On a late snowy winter night, a helicopter approached the compound with with 8 men dress in white, landed on the upper portion of Stony knob. The approach of the chopper was seen 2 miles away and the Marines were ready when it landed!

All 8 men were captured, with out a round being fired, every one concerned was glad the back up plan wasn't needed!

Wade, Marc, Larry, Gary Sr., Gary Jr., Brent, Roland and Hector were armed to the teeth with Kevlar covering their entire bodys, 4 choppers from the FBI in Ashville, with 8 heavily armed men, the 32 men weren't needed!

The 8 men that landed, were whisked away from Stony knob, with out an explanation!

Gary Sr. ask "Wade, what happened to the 8 men?" Wade smiled "Gary I'll check on them. But most likely, we'll never know! He was just glad, it was handled the way it was, with out any one being hurt or killed!"

Gary Sr. saw a lot of people go through Merlin's Door!

Some looked like business men, and some wore black junp suits and were heavily armed, some came back through the door! But most of them he never saw again and he often wondered what happened to them! But he Knew he would never know! And sometimes he worried about them, but for Merlin's Door, he knew it would always's be interesting or even intriguing!

And that he would meet some very interesting people, owning Merlin's Door!

And indeed he would! He would met Jeff Hobart and his son Larry Hobart in a place called Adamsville!

Jeff Hobart as Gary understood it, was the richest man in the World!

(DREAM TEAM)

And a sports figure, named Scotty Pepper, who as it turnout was the son of his older brother!

Scotty Pepper, who was touted to be the best athlete, that ever played the sports of Basketball, Baseball!

Russell Willow! He owned a flight charter service, a Korean fighter pilot a war hero!

(A FLIGHT TO NOWHERE)

Got lost in a storm, with 8 retired School teachers, they landed on an uncharted Island, they were stranded there for 2 years, and discovered a very interesting thing, The Fountain of Youth, only it wasn't a fountain it was a water fall!

(TEACHER)

And two very bright young men, Jake Treads and Don Hoover, after being coached by their 9 grade school Teacher's, turned out to be two of the brightest minds of the world, they taught, at MIT got their Phd's at 17 they were from Adamsville, and Gary thought he did have the most interesting Life!

(END)